ON THE EDGE
Stories at the Brink

ON THE EDGE
Stories at the Brink

Edited by Lois Duncan

Simon & Schuster Books for Young Readers

New York London Toronto Sydney Singapore

SIMON & SCHUSTER BOOKS FOR YOUNG READERS
An imprint of Simon & Schuster Children's Publishing Division
1230 Avenue of the Americas, New York, New York 10020

Book design by Steve Scott
The text of this book is set in Galliard.
Printed and bound in the United States of America
10 9 8 7 6 5 4 3 2 1
Library of Congress Cataloging-in-Publication Data
On the edge : stories at the brink / edited by Lois Duncan.
p. cm.
Summary: A collection of twelve stories by different writers and in different genres
in each of which a young person is physically and/or emotionally on the edge.
ISBN 0-689-82251-0
1. Children's stories, American. [1. Short stories.] I. Duncan, Lois, 1934-
PZ5.O555 2000
[Fic]—dc21
99-054262

For Debby,
Internet supersleuth,
with gratitude

Contents

Foreword

by Lois Duncan

I am the family photographer, and our photo albums contain pictures from every vacation we ever took, except one. That was our trip to the Grand Canyon, where I didn't take a single snapshot because I was in a state of such total panic that my hands couldn't hold the camera steady.

It started when we pulled into a parking area near the visitors' center, and before I knew what was happening, our five children (the youngest a three-year-old), antsy from being cooped up so long, poured out of our van and went racing to the edge of the drop-off.

And there wasn't any guardrail!

My first instinct was to leap out and go tearing after them, but I was terrified they might turn their heads to look back at me and go flying over the edge. I didn't even have the nerve to call out to them for fear that the littlest one in particular would respond to the challenge of "escaping from Mommy" by running even faster on her fat, unsteady little legs.

Immobilized by fear and helplessness, I just sat there, weeping and praying, and promising myself, *If I ever get*

*them back alive, I will never take them anywhere again
without leashes.*

Eventually all our children did return safely. But the horrifying vision of beloved bodies hurtling over the edge of that incredible precipice has haunted my dreams ever since.

When I set out to select a theme for a third collection of young adult stories to follow *Night Terrors* and *Trapped!*, I dug deep into my reservoir of personal horrors and came up with that particular nightmare. My stomach lurched at the memory, and I could feel the accelerated pounding of my heart in my fingertips.

The choice was made—this anthology would be titled *On the Edge.*

My irrational fear of heights had a strong effect upon my childhood and adolescence. I couldn't force myself to climb the ladderlike branches of our backyard oak tree, and so was automatically excluded from the group of neighborhood children who scampered like monkeys up to my brother's leaf-shrouded tree house. On ski vacations I was condemned forever to the bunny slope, from which I watched my adventurous classmates go soaring off on the chairlift, and although I was quite a good swimmer, I wouldn't join the swim team because competition would have required diving off the edge of the pool. Instead, I directed my energies toward composing poetry, writing articles for youth publications, and editing the school paper. My life career was shaped less by my strengths than my weakness.

Yet, although so much of my own youth was spent on

the edge of social activities and psychological challenges, I was nevertheless surprised when the majority of the award-winning writers from whom I solicited stories for this anthology interpreted the term "on the edge" in ways more emotional than physical. I had somehow expected to be flooded with tales about young heroes and heroines teetering on the edges of cliffs, inching their way along window ledges, or plunging in barrels over the edge of Niagara Falls. Instead, the only stories that involved the danger of physically falling were one about a boy in Hawaii trying to psych himself up for a dive from a fifty-foot ledge, and another about a soloist ballerina struggling to perform a dangerous routine on a stage smeared with Vaseline.

The majority of the writers whose stories appear on these pages have interpreted "on the edge" in ways I didn't anticipate.

Here you will meet Stevie, whose suicide attempt has placed her on the edge of a group of patients in a mental institution; Jeremy, who performs a tenuous balancing act between the physical world and the virtual world of the Internet; and Rachel, who exists on the edge of a family that rotates around the histrionics of her attention-hungry older sister.

But there are humorous stories here as well. Who can help smiling with empathy at the plight of love-struck Chris, on the edge of expressing his devotion to the girl of his dreams when his face erupts overnight with a volcanic zit? Or sympathizing with poor nerdy Donny, on the edge of being massacred by a 240-pound linebacker known as "the Doughnut," with nothing with which to defend himself except a pan of "Lithuanian pig brains"!

The most unusual story in this collection is also the most tragic, which is why I have chosen to place it at the end. Once readers have traveled the length of the elephant trench with seventeen-year-old May Moua as she flees the Pathet Lao patrol with her baby in her arms, they will want to call it a night—and sleep with the light on.

You are poised *On the Edge* of an extraordinary reading adventure.

Turn the first page and let the free fall begin!

At Bellweather Country Day School, where I go, or rather, where I used *to go—I don't think they let you come back once you've sliced up your arm in the girls' shower and gotten blood all over their disinfected white tiles—at that school for pussies, I scared kids. I have this look: I make my face very still and hard and I stare at you. I call it my Deranged Killer Look. It means* Leave me alone, get out of my way, I'm dangerous. *The kids at Bellweather believed it.*

Stevie in the Mirror

by Ellen Wittlinger

I can see right away it's a nuthouse. The caseworker doesn't even come inside, just turns me over to Hennessey and drives off before the steel door clunks shut behind me. At first I feel that burning behind my eyes, but I swallow a bunch of times to get it down inside. I haven't cried for years—no sense breaking my record now.

I stand there looking down this mile-long corridor while Hennessey flips through the papers on me. No pictures on the walls. Not a candy wrapper on the floor. Lights so dim you can barely see your own shoes. Way down the hall one of those heavy doors squeaks open and somebody laughs, loud, like nothing's funny, like *Listen to this one* or *I'll show you,* and then the door bangs closed and the sound is trapped inside again.

"Stephanie Ingersoll," he says, reading it off the page. It doesn't seem to be a name that interests him very much, but he sticks his hand out sideways and glances at me anyway. "I'm John Hennessey. I'm a counselor on the Girls' Unit. Since it's so late, we'll just find you a bed tonight. We can talk tomorrow."

I'm not about to shake his germy hand. And we can

3

put that talk off forever for all I care. "My name is Stevie," I tell him, to get that much straightened out. "Nobody calls me Stephanie."

"Okay. Stevie." He pretends to be an agreeable guy.

"This is a place for wackos, right?"

He laughs. "I know it looks formidable at night, but in the light of day—"

"I'm only a runaway, you know. I'm no fruitcake. All I did was run away from home!"

Hennessey—who's butt ugly and has these vein-popping muscles—he does this real slow look down my arm until his eyes bounce off the bandage on my wrist. Like that tells him all he needs to know. He doesn't have a clue.

"This is *so* not a big deal," I tell him. "It's practically a joke!"

"Tomorrow," he says. "We'll talk about it tomorrow."

What else can I do? He opens one of those heavy doors and I follow him into what I'm pretty sure is hell.

"Mama! Mama!" is all I hear when I come to the next morning. For a minute I don't remember where I am, and then, when I do, I think I might puke. There's a giant doll leaning over me, its big plastic eyes staring into mine, and somebody must have pulled her chain. Either that or this is an actual human nut.

"Mama!" she screams at me again.

"Oh, Patsy, you woke Stevie, didn't you?" A skinny woman with a chest like a bird comes running into the room where I'm quickly waking up. I'm not in one of the real bedrooms, just a room off the staff area that has a couch in it. Hennessey put me there last night so he wouldn't have to wake anybody. And now I know why— when the cuckoos are quiet, you don't want to get them riled up.

"I'm Carol Ann," the skinny woman says. "And this is Patsy." The giant Kewpie is rolling her eyes around in her head. Carol Ann tells me most of the other girls are having breakfast and I should wash up quickly and she'll take me over and introduce me to everybody. I can hardly wait.

Last night when I couldn't get to sleep, I was thinking about who all these crazy kids were going to be. I saw *One Flew over the Cuckoo's Nest* last year. I figure they'll all be drugged stupid, mumbling and slobbering. But at first when I walk into the cafeteria, it doesn't look that different from a regular high school—not as many kids and all girls, but they're just talking and shouting, no more out of control than most kids who've been locked up in classrooms all day. Of course these girls are locked up *all* the time, day and night.

At Bellweather Country Day School, where I go, or rather, where I *used* to go—I don't think they let you come back once you've sliced up your arm in the girls' shower and gotten blood all over their disinfected white tiles—at that school for pussies, I scared kids. I have this look: I make my face very still and hard and I stare at you. I call it my Deranged Killer Look. It means *Leave me alone, get out of my way, I'm dangerous.* The kids at Bellweather believed it.

Carol Ann gets me a breakfast tray and leads me over to a table of girls. I put on my D.K. Look so they get the idea who I am, and I sit down next to this pudgy person with stringy blond hair that hasn't seen shampoo in quite some time. Carol Ann makes the introductions.

"Girls, this is Stevie. She came in last night. This is Brooke, Rosemary, Latasha, and down at the end is Zena."

For some reason I look first at Zena, maybe because she's the farthest away from me. The Look is going full blast as I stare her down. But I can see immediately my eyes could be crossed and my tongue could be hanging out and this Zena wouldn't know the difference. I could be wagging my tail and barking.

Zena doesn't see me or anybody else. The pointer finger of her right hand is bobbing up and down like she's lecturing somebody, except nobody is sitting across from her and she isn't saying anything, just letting this dumb smile come and go across her face, like there's some joke being told inside her brain. My D.K. Look deteriorates into plain old staring.

"Hey, Brooke! Another A.S. You've got company!" Rosemary, the stringy blonde who's sitting next to me, points to my bandage.

"Shut up, asshole," is all Brooke says.

"What's an A.S.?" I don't want to sound dumb, but the Look is not impressing anybody, so I better figure out the lingo if I'm going to be here for a while.

"Attempted suicide. You're the third one this month. Not Miss Originality, though. Brooke here would never stoop to something as ordinary as a slit wrist, would you, bitch?"

Brooke doesn't say anything, but she gives me and Rosemary both a Deranged Killer Look that's a lot more convincing than mine.

"Whatayou always wanna start something for, Rosemary?" Latasha says. She takes her fork and bounces it across the table so it lands with a splash in Rosemary's milk glass. "Can't you ever just shut the fuck up? Or you need me to *help* you shut up?"

Nobody says anything for a minute, and my first spoonful of cereal is about halfway to my mouth when all of a sudden Rosemary jumps to her feet, picks up her breakfast tray, and throws it at Latasha. Damn! She bumps me and my food spills everywhere, plus I get some of the splashback from Rosemary's all over my best Pumpkins T-shirt.

But before I can even move over or figure out what to do next, Latasha is up and walking right across the table, going for Rosemary's neck. Her chair falls over and then she does too, and Latasha is on top of her on the floor, the two of them rolling around in puddles of orange juice and Cheerios.

It only takes a few seconds before Carol Ann and two other counselors drag them apart, but they're still swearing and spitting at each other. And when they pull them to their feet, I'm amazed to see that Rosemary is as pregnant as a big old cow. As pregnant as my stupid mother.

"Time-Out rooms for both of you," Carol Ann announces, and they're muscled out of the cafeteria in different directions, still yelling.

"You'll get used to it," Brooke tells me. "Everybody

in here fights all the time. Nothing else to do. Except sleep."

"You're in here because of your . . . A.S.?" I ask her.

"Yeah. You, too, I guess," she says.

"I'm mostly here because I ran away. After my dad died and my mom married this jerk, I couldn't hack it at home anymore. So they had me locked up. This thing"—I wave my wrist—"I didn't even mean it. It was just something to do."

Brooke gives a grunt. "Don't tell anybody *that*. Being a runaway is too wimpy. Play up the suicide thing."

"How did you do it? Your A.S."

"Hanging," Brook says, pulling out the neck of her T-shirt with one finger so I can see the meaty red scar, an ugly necklace. "I meant it."

"Most of the girls already have roommates," Carol Ann is explaining. "But there are beds available in Patsy's room and in Zena's."

Latasha, who got out of Time-Out before Rosemary because she didn't spend her first lockup hour screaming, hears what we're talking about.

"Come on, Carol Ann, you can't make her sleep in the same room with Patsy. Shit, this girl already tried to kill herself once!"

I'm not nuts about the choice either. Patsy's as creepy as they come, with her googly eyes spinning in circles, but Zena's a few sandwiches short of a picnic too.

Carol Ann puts her finger to her lips. "Latasha, please! Patsy will hear you!"

"Patsy doesn't know what the hell I'm talking about." She turns to me. "Patsy doesn't use the bathroom—you know what I'm saying? She just does it wherever. Her room smells like a sewer."

My jaw drops open. They'd make me sleep in a room with somebody who messes in her pants? I *am* in hell.

Carol Ann smiles one of those bullshit smiles grownups give you when they're pretending they're on your side. "Well, I'm thinking Zena might be the better choice anyway. She's making progress these days."

"Right," Latasha says, laughing. "Hey, let's get Zena to play her song for the new girl. What's your name again?"

I tell her, but she isn't really listening. She's yelling to Zena, who could be deaf for all the notice she takes. Zena's standing in the corner having another silent conversation with somebody; her mouth moves and that finger points, but there's nobody there to hear whatever she isn't saying. Latasha doesn't give up. She takes Zena by the arm and leads her to a couch. "Sit here," she commands. "I'm getting your guitar."

At the word *guitar*, Zena stops "talking" and sits quietly, waiting. Latasha is back in a minute with the guitar and hands it to Zena, who immediately puts the strap over her shoulder and gives a strum.

"Hey, everybody!" Latasha yells. "Zena's gonna sing her song." Then she turns to me and says, "You won't believe this. She wrote this herself."

Girls come out of their rooms, stop talking, gather around. Even the counselors stop pretending they have a lot of important work to do and look up.

Zena doesn't seem to even know we're there. She puts her head back and lets out a sound almost like a howl, except that it's beautiful. And then she sings her song. I've never heard anything like it.

OHHHH! Look into the mirror. Look into the wall.
  I can see your inside. I can see it all.
You cannot escape me, even if you try.
  What a little baby. Don't forget to cry.

OHHHH! My face is all muddy. You think that's a shame.
  Wash away the colors. Wash away the pain.
You will hold my hand and look into my eyes.
  Wash away the mother. Wash away the lies.

You might think there's one of me,
  a certain shape and size.
But one prefers the hello kiss,
  and the other loves good-byes.
Look into the mirror! Look into my eyes!
  You cannot see anything. But I'm alive!

OHHHH! Look into the mirror. Look into the wall.
  I can see your inside. I can see it all.
You cannot escape me, even if you try.
  What a little baby. Don't forget to cry.

She holds the last note until it *is* a cry. I can't explain what Zena sounds like: one minute like a shy little kid and the next like some real gutsy singer, Tori Amos or some-body. Most of the verses have kind of a simple melody, almost like a nursery rhyme, and then in the middle, the second time she says, "Look into the mirror," she starts to kind of wail. It's almost scary.

Everybody claps and hoots, but Zena doesn't even smile. She takes the guitar off and lays it on the couch, gets up, and walks back into the corner to finish that con-versation she was having with nobody. Or maybe with herself. My new roommate.

There's a Boys' Unit here too, which I figured there was, but I don't see any of them until today when we have Outdoor Recreation together. Which turns out to be baseball. God, I hate baseball. It seems like everybody else does too. Well, not everybody in the world, obvi-ously, maybe just us lunatics.

Not that I'm that much like the other kids. The girls are pretty equally divided between the totally gonzo types like Patsy and Zena, and the completely furious, violent ones like Rosemary and Latasha. I don't even fit in with the other two A.S. girls, both of whom really *wanted* to die. I guess I just wanted somebody to pay some atten-tion to me. At least that's what Hennessey gets me to admit right away in our first counseling session. Yawn. I'll say whatever I have to to get out of this place.

Anyway, the boys are just as crazy as the girls, but at first I don't think they are. I see this one guy, Victor, and I think he's really cute. We get picked for the same team, which means at least there's a lot of time to sit around on the bench and wait to get up to bat, and I manage to get myself sitting next to him. Rosemary's on the loose again and she's sitting on my other side, and she keeps up this constant laughing and blabbing, saying stuff like "What a cute couple" and "Stevie's got a boyfriend *already*!" I figure she's just jealous, so I ignore her.

Victor's not saying too much, but he's got the sweetest smile and he's really looking deep into my eyes, and I'm starting to think maybe this place won't be *so* bad, when Rosemary pokes her bony elbow into my side.

I turn around and glare at her. "What do you want!"

"I think Victor wants you to see something," she says, snorting with laughter. "He's got his horse out of the barn again." She motions toward his lap and I turn to see what the hell she's talking about, and then I see that Victor's got his fly open and his dick is actually lying out there in his lap!

I give a loud shriek and jump up and fall over Rosemary's big legs, which are stretched out around her huge stomach. I'm sitting there in the dust while Victor and Rosemary are in hysterics. Not for long, though. Woody, one of the Boys' Unit counselors, figures out right away what's going on and yanks Victor off the bench.

"Tuck it in, buddy," he tells him. "You're in Time-Out for the foreseeable future."

Carol Ann hightails it over to me. "You okay?"

"What the hell!" I say. "What's wrong with that guy?"

She takes me aside so the stupid game can continue. "Victor has a problem knowing how to act around women. He's gotten better, but when there's somebody new here, he likes to see if he can shock her. Sorry, Stevie. I should have warned you."

"Damn right you should have." My heart's banging away in my chest so hard it reminds me of the night my mother announced she was "bringing new life into the world," which was an even bigger shock to my system than this little deviant's pecker. My mother and that goofy Jake, so *thrilled* to be populating the planet with a tiny replica of themselves. I thought I was going to break into little pieces that night. Maybe I did. People are so damn dumb. All they think about is themselves. They don't even think what a terrible effect they're having on other people.

"What makes Victor do that?" I ask Carol Ann.

She shrugs. "A lot of kids here will do whatever it takes to be noticed."

"Well, that's a crappy way to get attention," I say. Although, when I think about it, none of the rest of us has such a great way either.

Zena's crying wakes me up, so I go over and shake her a little bit. She stops crying and looks at me, and for just a minute I can see somebody in there, somebody at home behind those eyes. But just for a minute, and then they get unfocused again and she turns onto her back to stare up at the ceiling.

I get back in bed, but now I'm awake. "How come you were crying?" I ask her. I don't usually bother to try to talk to Zena. On the first day we were roommates I figured out I was lucky to get her because she's quiet most of the time and she doesn't pay any attention to anybody anyway, so it's almost like not having a roommate at all. But I'd never heard her cry before, and I'd never seen her look back at me.

Of course she doesn't answer me, but for some reason, I start to hum her song. I've heard her sing it a few times now and it's hard to forget. It's the kind of song my mother would call "haunting." Zena doesn't move.

"Did your mother do something to you?" I ask her. "The part about 'wash away the mother, wash away the lies'—what does that mean?"

Still no sound from Zena, but she does roll over onto her side so that she's facing me. It's too dark and I'm too far away to see where her eyes are looking though.

"My mother is the reason I'm here too," I tell her. "She's having a baby with her new husband, who's an idiot. And she thinks I ought to be happy about it. I haven't been happy in four years—not since my dad died—I'm sure not going to be happy about *this*!"

I don't know if Zena understands a word I say—she's as quiet as a corpse—but for some reason, I really like talking to her. It seems to me she's listening, but not the way most of my friends listen for a few minutes and then get tired of it and say, "Wait till you hear what *my* mother did," and then they go off on some totally irrelevant story. Like my problem is in the same league with them not being allowed to have their own phone or something. Of course, everybody else at this place has such gigantic problems I don't bother to tell them mine. They'd think *I* was talking about telephones.

"Sometimes I think there's more than one of me

too," I tell Zena. "Is that what happened to you? All the pieces split apart?" The silence is fine. It's comfortable. I start to feel tired again. "Zena," I whisper to her. "If you need to cry again, go ahead. I won't stop you."

She doesn't cry anymore that night, but every few nights I hear her sobbing. I want to stop her because it makes me feel sad too, but I don't. You can't break a promise to Zena.

"Carol Ann tells me you and Zena are getting to be friends," Hennessey says during one of our regular late-afternoon appointments. He's my therapist. He's supposed to help me figure myself out before I'm sent back into the so-called *real* world. Here in therapy-world I sit in a comfy chair and pretend this old guy is my buddy. There's one of those trick mirrors on one wall of the room, as if there's somebody alive who doesn't know you can see through it from the other side. I like to pretend there's a mirror between me and Hennessey, too. That I can see him but he can't see me. Not really.

I give this little snort. "Friends? How can you be friends with somebody who doesn't talk? I mean, I like her all right. I like to hear her sing."

"You like her song?"

"Yeah. Everybody does. I wish she'd write some more."

"Her mother told me she wrote 'Look into the Mirror' right before her breakdown."

"If her mother even *knows*," I say.

"Why do you say that?" Hennessey wants to know.

I shrug. "The song doesn't make her mother sound like much of a saint."

Hennessey nods. "True, but then most mothers aren't saints."

"Maybe not, but most mothers *look* at their kids, most mothers have a *clue* about what's going on with their kids, most mothers don't *lie* to you!"

"Are we talking about *most* mothers now, or are we talking about *your* mother?" I love the way these shrinks get you tied up in your own knots. I decide not to answer that question. Hennessey thinks he's got me all figured out anyway, that everything I say and do is about my mother and what he calls her "betrayal."

"I think it might be a good time for your mother to come and visit, don't you? She's been asking to come, but I want you to feel you're ready."

This is one of the few things in my life I have any control over, especially here in the nuthouse. But as soon as I let her come, I give that up. *She's* in charge again.

"I don't want to see her. I'm not ready." There, I've made Hennessey frown.

When I wake up, Zena's sitting up in her bed already, staring at her hand.

"What are you looking at?" I ask her. I'm surprised when she turns her head toward me as though she might actually answer. There she is, behind her eyes, alive. Then she turns back to her hand.

I've been wondering lately how much of it is your own choice. Sometimes when I watch Zena or Patsy or even one of the wild girls, like Rosemary, I can imagine becoming just like them. I'd just need to *want* to. I'd just have to let go, give up, fall apart, go crazy. I think I could do it. It would be nice in a way. No responsibilities. I wouldn't even be expected to talk to Hennessey. I could go far away inside myself where my mother would never find me. I could hide. The problem is, once you let go, how do you come back? What if you get as lost as Zena?

"Are you hiding, Zena?" I ask her. "You don't have to hide from me."

"Hi, Victor." We're having a picnic with the Boys' Unit. By the pond. The one pretty place we're allowed to go, and not that often either. Victor hasn't tried anything on me since that one time. I think he mostly likes surprising people.

"Hi, Stevie. I heard Rosemary had a boy."

I nod. "This morning. She'll be back here tomorrow."

"She has to give it away, huh?"

I laugh. "They don't let fifteen-year-old nut jobs take care of babies. Pass me a tuna fish sandwich."

He hands me two. "Couldn't her mother have taken it or something? Until Rosemary got old enough?"

I shrug. "Her mother didn't do such a great job with Rosemary. The kid is better off adopted. They'll give him to some family who's just dying for a baby."

"I bet Rosemary's sad, though. It would be fun to have a baby, don't you think?"

"*Fun?* It's not about having fun, Victor. If you don't do a good job, you get a bunch of screwed-up kids like us."

He smiles. "What's so bad about us?"

Victor is cute, but he is really stupid.

This morning Latasha and a new girl, Wendy, got into a big fight, with Rosemary egging them on. For a change Carol Ann and the others weren't watching our every move—they were admiring their new coffeemaker—and before they got to them, Latasha had a broken nose and a big clump of Wendy's hair in her hand. There was blood all over the place and Patsy started wailing. I didn't even blame her—I felt like crap too.

I'm really getting tired of this place now. Two days ago Brooke ran away during a trip downtown. It's this big privilege to get to go, and the minute she gets out of the van she takes off. Of course they caught her right away, and now she's in Extended Time-Out, probably forever. I saw her when they brought her back. She looked like a Deranged Killer, but I'm pretty sure the person she was hoping to kill was herself.

I don't know who makes the choice, whether you make it yourself, or whether all the circumstances of your life decide for you. Or maybe it's a little of both. I just know I'm tired of being afraid of Rosemary, and I'm tired of feeling sorry for Patsy, and I'm tired of watching Brooke hate herself, and I'm tired of eating and sleeping and going to the bathroom when Carol Ann tells me to, and I'm tired of keeping Hennessey on the other side of the mirror.

I don't belong here. I never did. They only put me here because my mother was so scared. She thought one day she'd find me hanging from a branch of the Norway maple, like Brooke's mother did. I probably should tell her that whole wrist-cutting thing was a lie. If it's my choice, I think I'm ready to stop hiding. I just wish Zena was too.

"Tell my mother she can come and visit," I tell Hennessey.

"Are you sure?" he asks. Funny, the guy's not as ugly as he used to be.

I nod. "It doesn't seem like such a big deal anymore. So she has a new husband and a baby. It doesn't change who I am."

He's grinning. "I'm glad you can see that."

"Yeah. I figure when the kid gets old enough, like when Mom and Jake start bugging her, I'll tell her all about my dad, how cool he was."

Hennessey is thrilled. "That's wonderful, Stevie. You've done good work in here. I think you'll be able to go home soon."

"Can't wait," I say. "The food here sucks."

God, he's about ready to bust a gut. I bet he thinks *he* fixed me. *Please.* Get the guy a medal.

She seems better now in the mornings, not so much of that pointing and mumbling. Sometimes she stays in our room and plays chords on the guitar. I think she might be starting to write a new song. She sings so low I can't make out the words, but it's definitely a new tune. Whenever anybody comes in she stops, but she doesn't mind me. We're sort of friends.

"Zena, I have to tell you something," I say. She doesn't

look at me, but I know she's listening. "I think they're going to let me go home this week. I talked to my mother."

When I say the word *mother,* Zena looks at me. Her eyes are clear. Then she looks back at the guitar strings, plays a few chords.

"It wasn't that bad. I was really mad at her, you know? But then, when I actually saw her, it was okay. Like maybe part of it was in *my* head. She was really happy to see me. She says she wants me to come home, even though I messed up before. She's having her baby in a month. Which is weird, but I guess I can live with it." I almost don't say it and then I do. "Your mother is probably worse than mine, isn't she?"

Zena stops strumming and lays the guitar next to her on the bed.

"If you get better, you can come and visit me," I tell her. "Would you like that? You could sleep overnight in my room and we could pretend we were still roommates."

She's looking at me now. Her mouth moves, but she isn't talking to herself this time.

"What did you say?" I get up and sit next to her on her bed so I can hear better. "Did you say something to me?"

She leans over and whispers it. "Don't forget," she says.

"Don't forget what?" Zena is talking to me! I want her to tell me everything she knows! "You mean, don't forget *you*? I never will."

She leans in again. "Don't forget to cry," Zena says.

And so I do.

My senior year in college and the summer before, I worked in a residential mental health center for teenagers. My job was to be an observer, to sit on one of the two units (the boys and girls lived separately) and keep a record of the behaviors of whatever kids were being followed that day. I did indeed follow them, but I was never allowed to speak or interact with them in any way, the idea being that I wouldn't become emotionally involved with any of them, thereby skewing the data I was collecting.

Of course this was impossible. These kids were dying for people to pay attention to them, and my cohorts and I were a great challenge. Not speaking to them was the most difficult job I've ever had. I did smile at them sometimes, and I certainly had my favorites. The units, like those in "Stevie," housed kids with all sorts of problems: the violent, the suicidal, the completely dysfunctional. There was really a Zena; there was even a Victor. And then there was one girl, Donna, who'd done nothing more than run away from home. You could see the fear in her eyes the first day she arrived on the unit, and the thick wall she built up to get through the days in this strange, tough place.

Several years later, when I was in graduate school in another state, I was in a café with friends one afternoon when I saw a familiar young woman sitting at the counter. I kept looking at her, trying to place her. Before leaving, I approached her, and as she turned to look at me her face froze and I recognized her: Donna from the Girls' Unit.

For the minute I stood there mumbling my hellos, she (who had never heard my voice before) stared at me, and I knew she must have been flooded with awful memories.

I've thought of Donna for years, and now she's become Stevie. My fiction often starts like this, with someone I know, but probably not very well, so that the character is firmly grounded in my mind, but I can use my imagination to build the story.

I have written in many genres over the years: poetry, plays, and fiction. My young adult novels are *Lombardo's Law, Noticing Paradise, Hard Love,* and *What's in a Name. Gracie's Girl,* a middle-grade novel, will be published soon. I grew up in Illinois and have lived in Iowa and Oregon over the years, but now live in Massachusetts with my husband and two teenage children.

Jeremy no longer needed the mouse; he just willed himself to move. Mental control, wow! He'd read about it, but this was a first for him. On his monitor screen the terrain spread out before him, and then surrounded him. He saw thick, densely leaved trees with strange faces and bodies—animal and human—entwined in their branches. How could colors be dark and at the same time so vibrant? And the sounds! Frogs croaked, waves splashed, water dripped; he heard dim growls, subdued roars, the soft moaning of wind, but none of it was scary. It felt warm and dark and primitive, as though Jeremy knew this place, as though he'd been here long ago, when he was a baby waiting to be born.

"Move around, Jeremy the Jaguar," NetherMagus told him. "Explore my domain."

Nethergrave

by Gloria Skurzynski

"Beacon Heights Academy Lets Boys Excel!"

What a dumb motto. Did it ever occur to the school administrators, when they collected the thousand-dollar-a-month tuition fee per student, that maybe a boy didn't *want* to excel? Jeremy wished the motto was "Beacon Heights Academy Lets Boys Alone."

Each term every student in the academy had to participate in at least one after-school activity: drama, debate, the science fair, or a sport. Even if the student didn't board at the expensive, exclusive boys' school, but lived in town and went home every day after classes. Like Jeremy.

Jeremy had chosen soccer. Not because he liked it; not because he was any good at it; but because the coach was so determined to field a winning team that Jeremy knew he'd never get played—never in a real game, and rarely even in practice.

Until today. It was the last week of the spring term, which meant that to fulfill the school's requirement, Jeremy would have to play for at least one minute. And this would be a real game: the Beacon Heights Bulldogs against a tough team from across the valley, the Midvale

Marauders. All day long Jeremy had been wondering if he could fake stomach cramps or appendicitis, but the coach would never believe him. Jeremy might be a scared, skinny eighth-grade wimp, but he was a healthy one.

Didn't matter that he'd deliberately forgotten to bring his jersey and his shin guards to school: "Dig some out of the box," Coach barked. From the bottom of the smelly equipment box Jeremy pulled ratty shin guards and a sagging, much too large red jersey. When he ran out of the field house, a couple of his fellow eighth graders elbowed each other and snickered—maybe because of what Jeremy was wearing, but more likely because that was the way they usually reacted to him.

He sat on the bench so long his bony rump started to hurt. As the score seesawed—first the Beacon Heights Bulldogs were ahead, then the Midvale Marauders— Jeremy kept praying that the coach had forgotten about him. Not a chance. Coach was checking the list of boys from Beacon Heights, frowning at it, crossing off names with a pencil.

"Jeremy! You!" Coach barked. "Get out there. Replace the forward."

Shoulders hunched, Jeremy ran onto the field. Inside his head he was great at sports and games. On a computer he was unbeatable. He understood the geometry of basketball, baseball, football, and soccer, and he knew all the rules because he memorized things so easily. If only he'd had a reasonable amount of coordination, plus a little bit of muscle, he might have played soccer passably. But when Jeremy ran, his head and neck, arms and hands, legs and feet looked like a bunch of paper clips that had been shaken up in a bag: Hooked together haphazardly, they stuck out at all kinds of weird angles.

The coach blew his whistle. Jeremy stumbled forward, trying to get into the open so one of his teammates could pass him the ball. As if they would. All of them knew that a pass to Jeremy would mean losing the ball to the Midvale Marauders. Yet, there it was—the soccer ball—and it looked like it was coming right at him! He got a foot on it, lost it, and in the mayhem of other boys' arms and legs, noticed the ball rolling loose. Running after it, he started dribbling toward the goal.

Unbelievable! He was moving that soccer ball down the field and it appeared he might even kick a goal, his first in his whole two years at Beacon Heights. Concentrating, pumped with adrenaline, he didn't notice that his teammates weren't anywhere near him. No one was helping him, he had no protection, no chance to pass, but it didn't matter, because Jeremy was going to do it! Make a goal! He pulled his eyes off the ball just for a second, barely in time to notice that the goalie was—a Beacon Heights Bulldog! Frantically, the goalie waved his arms and shook his head, but not in time to stop Jeremy's foot, which had already begun its trajectory to kick the ball into the net. A perfect kick! Jeremy scored!—for the Midvale Marauders. He'd kicked a goal at the wrong end of the field, scoring a point for the opposing team.

Coach looked ready to burst a blood vessel as he screamed at Jeremy to get off the field. The Marauders looked ready to bust a gut, punching one another in hilarity while they laughed themselves stupid. The Bulldogs—well, Jeremy knew what would be coming later from his teammates. He was used to it.

At school he was constantly getting tripped in the halls, in the aisles, on the gym floor, in the locker room. The other guys had raised tripping Jeremy to an art form. He figured that today, since he'd blown the game, he'd be in for a world-class tripping. He was right. In the locker room three of his teammates choreographed it perfectly: As one tripped him, another bumped Jeremy's left shoulder from behind, while a third boy, in front of him, shoved Jeremy's right shoulder, whipping him around so he pitched facedown onto a bench.

"Jeremy, grab a towel and hold it under your nose," the coach bellowed in disgust. "You're getting blood all over the floor."

The bleeding stopped, but the swelling didn't. Afterward, walking home, Jeremy hung inside the late-afternoon shadows so no one could notice him. He hoped his mother wouldn't get home until the swelling had gone down at least a bit. If she saw it, she'd just sigh and shake her head in that pitying way, wondering how she'd ever produced such an incompetent son. But his mother rarely got home before eight or nine at night. Usually she had dinner with a client.

Jeremy didn't have to worry about his father seeing his swollen nose, since his father never saw him at all. Once in a while Jeremy would find his father's picture in *Forbes* magazine or in the business section of *U.S. News and World Report,* which listed him as one of the computer industry's rich, triumphant successes. He owned a corporation that designed printed circuit boards. With Bill Gates and Steve Wozniak and Steve Jobs, Jeremy's father had been in the right place at the right time when the computer revolution took off.

Not once since his parents' divorce twelve years ago had Jeremy and his father come face-to-face. Like clockwork, though, every year on Jeremy's birthday a van would back up to the front door of his house. Two techno-brains would carry in a brand-new computer with the most powerful chip produced that particular year, with the greatest amount of memory, the fastest modem, and the biggest monitor screen. They'd install the new computer and transfer all Jeremy's previous programs onto its hard drive, then pack up last year's computer to haul it away.

Did his father actually *order* the world's best PC each year for Jeremy's birthday? Did he speak the words "I want a top-of-the-line personal computer system delivered to my son"? Or was it just a digital instruction, programmed to come up automatically on the screens of the two techno-brains? It didn't matter. Equipment like that would have made Jeremy the envy of his friends, if he'd had any.

He unlocked the front door. Even though he was hungry, he didn't open the refrigerator, because the clock showed 4:05. He was fifteen minutes late. He'd wasted too much time skulking in the shadows on the way home. Hurrying into his room, he threw his books onto his bed, dropped his jacket on the floor, and turned on his computer.

On the screen, he checked his contact list. The others were already online, their names highlighted in blue:

Hangman
PrincessDie
Dr.Ded

When he clicked on his own online name, Xtermin8r, the screen split from three to four boxes in the chat module he shared with his online friends.

"You're late, X," Hangman typed, the words flowing into the right-hand box on the top of the screen. X was what they called Jeremy, because *Xtermin8r* took too long to type.

"Sorry," Jeremy typed back in his own box; he automatically got the one at top left.

"We didn't do the jokes yet. We waited," PrincessDie typed.

"So begin now." The words from Dr.Ded marched slowly across his quarter of the screen. He wasn't a very fast typist.

The four of them met online every day after school. They'd first come across one another in a music chat room dedicated to the Grateful Dead. Eventually, after a couple of weeks of meeting in that much larger chat group, they'd decided to form their own module, limited to the four of them. Calling themselves the DeadHeads, they chose online names that had to do with death, and began every afternoon's chat session with "dead" jokes.

PrincessDie: *Okay, here goes. Question: What does a song-writer do after he dies? Answer: He de-composes.*

Hangman: *Good one. Here's mine. Question: What does a walking corpse call his parents? Answer: Mummy and Dead-y.*

Dr.Ded: *Ha ha. Q: How do you kill a vegetarian vampire? A: Put a steak through his heart.*

Hangman: *All right!!!! Your turn, X.*

With all that had happened that day, Jeremy hadn't thought up a dead joke. He hesitated, then typed, *"Q: What kind of pants do ghosts wear? A: Boo jeans."*

Hangman: *Bad one, X.*

Dr.Ded: *Your joke stinks, X. It's from preschool. You better do better than that.*

PrincessDie: *Yeah--you better--do better--the Grateful Dead could have made a song out of that.*

Hangman: *Your penalty, X--find two excellent dead jokes for tomorrow. I mean excellent.*

Jeremy was the fastest typist in the group. His fingers flew across the keys as he entered, *"I apologize, guys. Today was a busy day for me. I played in a soccer tournament at school, and I kicked the winning goal. Everyone in the stands jumped up, and they were yelling my name and cheering--so cool! Then my mom and dad took me out for burgers and fries to celebrate. That's why I logged on late today. Even this morning I was too busy to look up dead jokes. In gym they announced I'm gonna be the captain of the wrestling team."*

If his online friends only knew it, that was the biggest joke Jeremy could have possibly told them.

Now he typed even faster, trying to get it all in before the three other DeadHeads started up again. *"After they made me captain, the wrestling team guys poured a bottle of*

Evian water over my head. They said it should have been champagne, except we'd all get kicked out of school if they did that. So I was wet all over and I had to borrow a hair dryer from Miss Jepson--she's my French teacher and she's a real babe and she likes me--like, more than just a regular student. I think she'd go out with me if I asked her."

He'd told his online friends he was a high school junior. They thought he was a star athlete and a student-body officer and a lot of other things Jeremy was careful to keep track of so he wouldn't forget what he'd told them. To keep his lies straight, he printed out each day's online chat and saved the hard copies in a three-ring binder.

Hangman: *Gotta go now.*

Jeremy typed, "*Already? I just got here.*"

Hangman: *Gotta write a heavy-duty report for earth science.*

PrincessDie: *Me, too, gotta go. To meet a guy. Don't freak, Xtermin8r. I know you want to be my guy, but you're in Ohio and I'm in Oregon.*

In real life—IRL—Jeremy lived in Pasadena, California, but his father had been born in Ohio, so that's where he told his online friends he was from.

Dr.Ded came on then, typing even more slowly than usual.

Dr.Ded: *I'm outta here too, guys. Gonna do some major surfing-- the ocean kind. Surf's up too great to waste. Find you all tomorrow. Don't forget, X, you owe us two *good* jokes.*

On the screen, the names of his three friends turned green: The color change meant they'd gone offline. Then their boxes disappeared, leaving Jeremy's words alone on the screen.

It wasn't that they'd deserted him, he told himself. He'd been late—they'd probably chatted for quite a while before he got there. At least they hadn't done the dead jokes until he logged on. Why hadn't he come up with a better dead joke? Maybe they didn't like him today because he'd typed such a rotten joke. He felt himself sinking into his expensive padded office chair, weighed down as if he'd swallowed a heavy paving brick. His last words, "Already? I just got here," vibrated on the screen.

He sighed. Might as well print out the day's chat and file it in his binder. His cursor was on its way to the "Print" command when his name appeared on the screen.

Jeremy, followed by a question mark. One of his online buddies must be back.

He typed, *"I'm here."*

More words followed: *Click your middle mouse button, Jeremy. And turn on your microphone.*

When he clicked the mouse, the screen exploded with color—swirling waves of such brilliant hue he raised his hand to shade his eyes. "Hey, what is this?" he asked out loud into the mike.

A man's voice, deep and mellow, answered through the audio system, "Welcome to Nethergrave, Jeremy."

On Jeremy's twenty-one-inch monitor screen, with its sixteen million colors, a whirling vortex appeared, so three-dimensional he felt he could dive into it. Never had he seen color this intense, or screen resolution so high. It was more vivid than an Imax theater movie.

He stared, unblinking, until it seemed he was being sucked inside the vortex. Wow! What fantastic imaging, he thought, but then he quit thinking so he could give himself entirely to the illusion of flying through the whorls. They rotated around him; he was a weightless body caught in a fast-spinning, kaleidoscopic tunnel. As he neared the end of the vortex he saw the face of a man growing larger and larger until it filled the screen.

A real face? Probably not. It looked more like a mask. The black eyebrows angled upward, too symmetrical to be natural. Beneath the cheekbones, green-tinged shadows formed triangles with the apex at the bottom, just touching the corners of the too-red, too-smiling mouth. Black hair peaked in the center of the man's forehead, then swept back as sleekly as if it were molded plastic.

"Who are you?" Jeremy asked.

His lips moving in not quite perfect synchronization, the man answered, "I'm NetherMagus. You've entered my domain."

Jeremy glanced at the Internet address on the top of his screen—http://nethergrave.xx/. He'd never heard of a domain extender called "dot xx," but then, new ones got added to the Internet every day.

The man—or the mask—continued, "Before you come any farther into Nethergrave, Jeremy, select a persona for yourself. Your very own avatar. You can choose whoever you would most like to be. Or I should say, *whatever* you would most like to be."

One by one, images emerged on the screen, not simply masks like NetherMagus's, but full-body images: a unicorn; a princess wearing a tall, peaked cap with a filmy scarf wafting from it; a Roman soldier with a bronze breastplate; a falcon; a Medusa who had hair of writhing snakes; a Japanese warrior, his samurai sword raised as if to strike; a monk with a hood shadowing his face so that no feature showed, only glowing eyes; a sinewy jaguar that loped gracefully, its muscles bunching beneath a sleek, tawny coat that gave off shimmers of light like ripples of sheet lightning on a hot midnight—

"That one," Jeremy said, pointing. "The jaguar."

Immediately he saw clawed feet running just ahead of his line of vision. They were his feet, because he was the jaguar, looking out through gleaming, molten jaguar eyes. Shifting his glance from side to side, he saw whiskers projecting outward from the edges of his face, and a moist black nose—he had to almost cross his eyes to see the nose in front of his face, but there it was: a jaguar nose. When he tried wrinkling it, the muzzle curled as if in a snarl. And it didn't hurt like his real nose did. But wait! His real nose had stopped hurting; had it actually become the animal nose? It didn't matter—this was a fantastic role-playing game, with a great first-person point of view. He felt as if he were inside the jaguar, looking out through its eyes.

"It's so cool!" he exclaimed. "I never knew a game existed with graphics and special effects like these. Can I download it so I can have it on my hard drive?"

Still smiling, NetherMagus merely answered, "There's much more to see. Come forward."

Jeremy no longer needed the mouse; he just willed himself to move. Mental control, wow! He'd read about it, but this was a first for him. On his monitor screen the terrain spread out before him, and then surrounded him. He saw thick, densely leaved trees with strange faces and bodies—animal and human—entwined in their branches. How could colors be dark and at the same time so vibrant? And the sounds! Frogs croaked, waves splashed, water dripped; he heard dim growls, subdued roars, the soft moaning of wind, but none of it was scary. It felt warm and dark and primitive, as though Jeremy knew this place, as though he'd been here long ago, when he was a baby waiting to be born.

"Move around, Jeremy the Jaguar," NetherMagus told him. "Explore my domain."

With his shoulders and haunches swiveling powerfully, Jeremy stalked the rain forest, feeling every muscle as it contracted in his perfectly coordinated body. He was passing cleanly through odd, swaying creatures: a clown head on a seal's body; a mermaid on a swing made of moss; a pool with dozens of submerged birds, their feathers changing colors as they fluttered beneath the water. "I gotta E-mail your URL address to my friends," he cried. "They'll freak over this!"

"Your friends, the DeadHeads," NetherMagus said, not as a question but as a statement.

"How'd you know?"

"I'm a Magus; I know things," the mask answered. "I know about PrincessDie—the only one of your group who is what she says she is: a pretty girl, an excellent student. But she's growing bored with the rest of you, Jeremy. Tomorrow she'll leave you, because she has outgrown your little chat quartet."

Figures swam past Jeremy—exotic gargoyles and pale spheres as transparent as air. "Then I guess it'll just be us three guys," he answered, shrugging, surprised at how mighty his shoulders felt in the shrug. "Just Dr.Ded and Hangman and me."

NetherMagus murmured, "Hangman will be lost to you too, Jeremy, although not because he wants to be. His school grades are so bad that tonight his parents will remove the computer from his room. He will be—as you young people say—grounded. From the Internet. Until his grades improve, which they will not, because very soon he will join a street gang."

"You couldn't possibly know all that stuff," Jeremy said scornfully as his claws—no, his fingernails—dug into soft turf. No! Dug into the keyboard. This was a game, the most incredible game he'd ever played, but still a game.

His father's people must have programmed it into the computer's hard drive months ago, as a surprise for Jeremy, just before they delivered the new computer on his birthday. They probably figured Jeremy would stumble onto the game right away. Long before this.

Maybe, during all these months, his dad had been hoping to hear from him. Waiting for Jeremy to thank him. What if he'd had the game designed especially for Jeremy and was right now sitting expectantly in that big office Jeremy had once seen in a picture in *Newsweek,* just waiting for a phone call from the son he'd abandoned twelve years earlier—

Or maybe—not.

"Come back, Jeremy," NetherMagus urged gently. "Don't you want to know about Dr.Ded?"

"No!" When Jeremy shook his head violently, his ears moved in an odd way, as though they were flexible and had grown higher on his head. "Wait, I guess I do. Yes."

NetherMagus told him, "Dr.Ded has deceived you far more than you've deceived any of the others."

"Me? Deceive? Oh, I guess you mean those stories I make up online. You know about them?"

"I know everything about you, Jeremy. I know that today you disgraced yourself on the soccer field—a truly humiliating experience! But back to Dr.Ded. He isn't a boy like you. He isn't a boy at all. He's a fifty-two-year-old stroke victim. He can't walk."

"Wrong! He said he was going surfing this afternoon."

The deep voice remained gentle. "He's confined to his bed, Jeremy. Soon he'll be moved to a nursing home that doesn't have an Internet connection. And you'll be all alone, Jeremy, abandoned by each of your online friends."

Jeremy swallowed, but his throat made an animal sound like a whimper. "What'll I do?"

The red smile on the face, or mask, grew even wider, as though it had been sliced by the samurai warrior's sword. "Stay with us, Jeremy. Live forever in Nethergrave. Here no one will ever abandon you, I promise."

"How do I get to Nethergrave?"

"You're already there!"

• • •

"Jeremy?" The call came from outside his bedroom door.

After a moment the door opened and his mother called again, "Jeremy? Sorry I'm so late—I was with a really important client. I just checked the refrigerator and you didn't eat your dinner. Why not?"

Entering the room, she peered around for her son. His schoolbooks had been flung on the bed, and his computer monitor glowed, but Jeremy wasn't there.

She bent down to pick up his jacket from the floor. As she straightened she caught sight of the computer screen. On it a jaguar raced through a clearing in a rain forest, its lean, sinewy body stretching and compressing as it ran, its tail soaring proudly. Struck by the animal's power and the incredible gracefulness of its movements, she stood quiet for a minute, staring, pressing Jeremy's jacket against her chest. The image of the jaguar moved her in a way she didn't understand. The animal was more than beautiful; it looked—triumphant!

She wondered if Jeremy had seen it.

Gloria Skurzynski

As a lover of computers and virtual reality, I've experienced every kind of VR available in the U.S. today. In decades to come, as digital technology grows more sophisticated, I believe there may be a seamless integration between the world we live in and the computer-generated virtual world. Then we'll all be faced with the choice of where we want to spend time—in the often harsh real world, or inside virtual reality, where we can choose who or what we become, as Jeremy does in "Nethergrave."

Will Jeremy ever decide to leave Nethergrave? I'm not sure.

Gloria Skurzynski is the author of two novels dealing with virtual reality: *Cyberstorm* and *Virtual War.* She also has written a number of nonfiction books on technology, including *Almost the Real Thing,* a book about computer simulation that won the Science Writing Award from the American Institute of Physics. For more information about Ms. Skurzynski's forty fiction and nonfiction titles, her background, and her many national awards, log on to her Web site at http://redhawknorth.com/gloria/.

Ms. Skurzynski lives in Salt Lake City, Utah, with her husband, Ed, a rocket scientist. They're the parents of five grown daughters, all of them computer literate (one of them is an electrical engineer and another a computer engineer). Through the Internet the family members stay closely connected, although they live far apart today in widely separated regions of the country.

He stared at me for a long minute, his hand slowly kneading my shoulder. "If you're lying, you'd better tell me now. I might just hurt you a little bit."

I gave the Boy Scout sign. "I swear, Doughnut. I'm bringing Lithuanian fried brains."

He grunted, still looking suspicious, and let me go.

I made it to the street on wobbly knees and started the walk home past the grade school and down the hill into the Third Ward. What had I done? If I didn't show up tomorrow with Lithuanian fried brains, I'd better show up with a doggone good excuse. Or else Doughnut was going to hurt me a lot more than a little bit.

Pig Brains

by Alden R. Carter

I was headed for the outside doors and the fall afternoon when a voice behind me boomed, "Hey, Shadis!"

I turned, smile fixed, resigned to taking the usual load of garbage from my favorite Neanderthal: the Doughnut. Now, Doughnut's a big guy, about six four and maybe 260, making him a foot taller and about 120 pounds fatter than I am. Fortunately, the brain that knocks around inside his massive skull is inversely proportional to his overall size. Put another way, I'm twice as smart. Which is handy. "Hey, Doughnut," I said.

He flopped a python-thick arm around my shoulders. "When you coming out for football, Donny? I could use a blocking dummy." He guffawed. Nitwit.

"Maybe next year," I said, and changed the subject. "What are you bringing to O'Brien's class tomorrow?"

"Huh?" he said.

"Food, Doughnut. We're supposed to bring something that reflects our ethnic heritage." *Which in your case is probably raw mastodon,* I thought, but didn't say.

"Oh, yeah," he said. "I nearly forgot. My ma's going

43

to make some doughnuts. We're German, and Germans eat a lot of doughnuts."

"Do they?" I said, to be polite.

"Yeah. At least my family does." He grabbed a fistful of his belly with typical lineman's pride. "Doughnuts put lead in our pants so we can block better. Coach O'Brien loves how I block. And he loves my mom's doughnuts, too."

"Really?" I said.

"Yep. I brought six dozen to practice just last week. They were all gone in five minutes."

"Do tell?" I said.

"Yep. So, who else is bringing food tomorrow?"

"It's you, me, and Melinda Riolo this week."

"Melinda? Hey, you kinda liked her last year, didn't you?"

"She's okay," I said.

"I think she thinks you're a nerd." He laughed.

Well, she thinks you're a baboon! So we're even, jerk. "Makes no difference to me," I said.

He grinned, knowing better. "Yeah, right. So, what are you bringing?"

"Brains," I said. "Lithuanians eat a lot of brains."

He stared at me. "You're kidding!"

"Nope. Calf brains, sheep brains, goat brains, all sorts of brains."

He let his arm drop from my shoulder. "That's gross."

"Not really. I like pig brains best. They've got kind of a nutty flavor."

Suddenly his hand was back on my shoulder, and it wasn't friendly. He turned me to face him, his eyes mean.

"You're putting the Doughnut on, man. I don't like it when people do that. It's like they think I'm stupid or something."

But you are, Doughnut. You are. I just wish you weren't so big. "I'm not putting you on, Doughnut. I swear."

He stared at me for a long minute, his hand slowly kneading my shoulder. "If you're lying, you'd better tell me now. I might just hurt you a little bit."

I gave the Boy Scout sign. "I swear, Doughnut. I'm bringing Lithuanian fried brains."

He grunted, still looking suspicious, and let me go.

I made it to the street on wobbly knees and started the walk home past the grade school and down the hill into the Third Ward. What had I done? If I didn't show up tomorrow with Lithuanian fried brains, I'd better show up with a doggone good excuse. Or else Doughnut was going to hurt me a lot more than a little bit.

The only sane, logical thing to do was to come up with a good excuse. But the more I thought about it, the more I really wanted to bring fried brains. I wanted to gross Doughnut out. I mean, the guy grossed me out just by being alive. Now it was my turn.

There really is a recipe for fried brains in the Lithuanian cookbook my mom has. She wrote away for it last spring so she could make a special dinner for my grandpa's eightieth birthday. I helped her pick the menu: "Hey, Mom, here's one we could try. Lithuanian fried brains. Soak the brains overnight in a pan of water in the refrigerator, then—"

"Stop," she said. "I don't want to hear it."

"But, Mom! Maybe he had them growing up. Maybe he's been longing for some fried brains ever since he left Lithuania."

"Believe me, he hasn't. He's a finicky eater. It drove your grandma nuts."

"Aw, Mom—," I whined.

"No brains! Find something else."

By the time I got home the sheer brilliance of my inspiration had produced some blind spots in my usually acute vision. Except for twenty or thirty sound, sane reasons, I couldn't see why I shouldn't bring fried brains. Oh, there were a few complications—like where to get the basic ingredient—but that was minor stuff. I could make this happen.

I called Lerner's Meat Market and asked if they had any brains. Mr. Lerner laughed. "No, I haven't seen brains on sale in thirty years. Nobody around here cooks brains. Maybe in Albania or someplace, but not central Wisconsin."

"Rats," I muttered.

"Nope, we don't have them, either. You might try Albertson's Supermarket, though. They might have rats."

"Ha, ha," I said. "Very funny."

"We try. What do you want the brains for?"

"A science project."

"Oh. Well, you might try the stockyards over in Stuart."

How was I supposed to get to Stuart without a car, a license, or a gullible parent? (My mom was decidedly

ungullible, my dad permanently absent without leave.)
"Do you suppose Albertson's might have some brains?" I
asked.

"You could ask, but I'd bet a thousand to one against."

"Thanks, Mr. Lerner."

"Sure enough. Good luck."

I slumped in the chair. No brains, no gross-out of the
Doughnut. Rats and double rats. (Or words to that effect.)
But the idea wouldn't let go, and I had my second inspiration of the day. Remember the Halloween game where
squealing kids pass the pieces of Frankenstein's monster
from hand to hand under a sheet: grapes for the eyes, a
carrot for the nose, pepper slices for the ears, *spaghetti for
the brains? Shadis,* I told myself, *you are brilliant.*

I pedaled my mountain bike down to Albertson's
and inspected the pasta selections. I finally decided on
fettuccine, although I was briefly tempted by some green
linguine.

Mom was meeting a client for supper and my sister was
studying at a friend's, so I had the kitchen to myself. Good
thing, because making some passable brains out of fettuccine took quite a bit of experimentation. I finally managed
what I thought was a pretty good facsimile by cooking the
noodles al dente, rolling them in cornmeal, and frying
them in some oil. I drained them on paper towels, stuffed
them into a loaf pan, and stuck it in the refrigerator.

By then I was on a pretty good roll. *A dip,* I thought.
We need some brain dip. I searched the refrigerator and
found half a bottle of cocktail sauce. I poured it into a neu-
tral container and wrote "Lithuanian Brain Dip" on a label.

Nah, I could do better than that. I tore it off and wrote "Cozzackakus: Blood of the Cossacks." Much better.

Digging in the refrigerator at breakfast the next morning, my sister yelped, "Oh, gross!"

Mom looked over Amy's shoulder. "What on earth?"

"Don't touch," I said. "Social studies project."

"What could this possibly have to do with social studies?" Mom asked.

"Really!" my sister said.

"I meant science," I said. "You don't want to know any more."

"You've got that right," Mom said. "Just get it out of my refrigerator."

By this time the dazzle of my idea had faded considerably and I was having some decidedly unpleasant second thoughts. Playing a joke on Doughnut was dangerous enough, but getting caught by Mr. O'Brien might be even worse. Mr. O'Brien doesn't fit the stereotype of a football coach. He doesn't have a big belly, he doesn't glower a lot, and he doesn't think football is the most important thing in the world. He thinks social studies is. He expects a lot, even from Doughnut, who sits in the back of the class trying to look interested. (Doughnut thinks O'Brien is God. Or just about.)

Mr. O'Brien pegs the needle on his hyper meter at least four or five times a day. He crashes around the room, slapping his pointer on maps, globes, and time lines. He pounds his fist on his desk, climbs on his chair, playacts at being this or that historical figure, even beats his head against the wall if that's what it takes to make a point. In other words, he's a heck of a teacher. But he isn't someone to mess with, and I was beginning to wish I was bringing Lithuanian sponge cake or something. Maybe I'd tell everybody that I'd brought Lithuanian cornmeal-coated fried noodles. Big delicacy, if you're into that kind of thing. Then I'd lie like crazy to Doughnut and hope that he only broke a couple of my bones.

Melinda Riolo didn't bother to go to her desk but marched right to the front of the room with her casserole dish. She stood there, tapping her foot, while Mr. O'Brien finished the roll. He smiled at her. "All right, Miss Riolo, go ahead."

She uncovered the dish and tilted it for everybody to see. "I brought eggplant parmigiana, which I like because it doesn't have a lot of calories. Since I lost all that extra weight last year in junior high, I don't eat a lot of the fattening stuff Italians like. I mean all the cheese and stuff. But this is pretty good. Enjoy." She set down the dish and marched to her desk across the aisle from mine. My heart bumped a couple of times with longing.

Doughnut swaggered to the front. He opened a big plastic pail of greasy sugar doughnuts. "They're really good," he said. "My mom fries 'em in real lard."

Melinda muttered, "Oh, charming. Now they're an extra five hundred calories." She eyed me narrowly. "You're being quiet today. Did you forget to bring something?"

"No, I've got it right here in the bag."

Pig Brains   **49**

"What is it?"

"Brains," I said.

"You're putting me on!"

I looked at her and couldn't lie. "Yeah, but don't tell anybody else. It could cost me about sixteen broken bones."

Doughnut finished telling how he could put away a dozen doughnuts straight from the boiling deep fryer. "Two dozen if they're small. They don't call me the Doughnut for nothing!" He grinned, using both hands to grab fistfuls of his belly. People laughed, and he swaggered back to his desk.

I took a deep breath, followed it with a short prayer, and stumbled confidently to the front of the class. I whipped the towel from the top of the loaf pan. "Ladies and gentlemen, boys and girls, these are Lithuanian fried brains. They're an old delicacy in traditional Lithuanian homes. When we're up at my grandpa's, we play a lot of pinochle. And while we play, we usually have popcorn, chips, or fried brains."

I prodded at the greasy tangle with a finger. Jeez, it was obvious they were noodles. Even Doughnut must have guessed by now. "It's kind of hard to find brains to fry sometimes. Sheep and goat brains are supposed to be the best, but there just aren't many sheep and goats around here. Calf brains are easier to find and they're really good. But I like pig brains best and that's what I brought today."

Up to this point I'd been too nervous to look directly at my classmates. But now I chanced it and was greeted by a lot of open mouths, screwed-up noses, and generally horrified expressions. Doughnut was absolutely gray. Good Lord, they believed me! I took a breath and put the accelerator to the floor. "Now, when we get the brains, we soak them overnight in a big pan in the refrigerator. It's kind of a good thing to remember they're in there. Otherwise, the next time you open the refrigerator, it's— *whoa*—Frankenstein's laboratory! But"—I shrugged— "you kind of get used to that sort of thing around my grandpa's house."

I dug into the tangle, separated a sticky wad of three or four noodles, and held it up. "The next morning we slice the brain and it falls apart into these sort of floppy, wormlike things." (There were some very satisfying groans. Doughnut had gone from gray to ashen.) "We roll them in cornmeal and fry them in oil. We drain them on some paper towels and then put them on the table in a big bowl. Brains are really best served hot, but they're still good cold. Like popcorn's good hot or cold."

I headed the wad of noodles toward my mouth, then pulled it back at the last second. "Whoops, I almost forgot. There's also the dip my mom makes from an old recipe my grandma brought from the old country. It's called *Cozzackakus,* which means 'blood of the Cossacks.' I asked my grandpa about the name and he said it's because Lithuanians don't like Cossacks, who used to be these real tough bandit types who raided a lot. My grandpa says not even Cossacks like Cossacks that much, so—"

Mr. O'Brien interrupted. "This would be an example of an ethnic prejudice, class. As we discussed, many older people have them. Go ahead, Don. This is just great."

"Ah, thanks. Anyway, I'm not sure my grandpa ever actually knew any Cossacks, but that's how the sauce got its name. So here's how you eat pig brains." I dipped the noodles in the shrimp sauce, stuck them in my mouth, and chewed. They were terrible, but I grinned. "This is a really good batch. Pig brains are just so much better than calf or beef. Did I mention beef brains? The butchers stopped selling them because people started worrying about mad cow disease. But my grandpa says all Lithuanians are already pretty crazy, so they probably wouldn't get any worse if they caught it. So, anyway, who'd like to try some Lithuanian fried brains?"

Nobody moved for a long minute. Then Melinda stood and strode to the front of the class. She gave me a look that was at least half glare. "I bet these are fattening as all get-out."

"I don't know, Melinda. Maybe a little."

She plucked a few noodles from the pan, dipped them in the cocktail sauce, and popped them in her mouth. She chewed and then shrugged. "Not bad. Could use some salt, maybe."

Mr. O'Brien jumped up. "Okay, everybody line up. You know the rule: Everybody's got to try everything, unless you've got a genuine, doctor-certified food allergy." He rubbed his hands together. "This is great! Just great. This is what we want. Something unusual. Something really authentic. Come on, everybody. Line up. Paper plates and spoons are right here. Don and Melinda, go ahead. No standing on ceremony here."

When we were back at our desks, Melinda glared at the doughnut on her plate. "I'd rather have brains." She leaned over and started to whisper, "You were kid—"

"Hold on, Doughnut!" Mr. O'Brien shouted. "You missed the brains. No cheating."

Doughnut grinned sheepishly and dug a few noodles from the pan.

"Don't forget the blood sauce, Doughnut," I called. "Makes them even better."

Leaning against his desk, Mr. O'Brien was digging into a big serving of brains. He smacked his lips. "You know, Don. If I didn't know better, I'd swear these were noodles."

I almost choked on a bite of eggplant but managed a weak smile. "Yeah, they're kind of similar, aren't they?"

"Sure are. What do you think, Doughnut?"

Doughnut was sitting at his desk, staring at his plate. He looked up pleadingly at Mr. O'Brien, who gave him a now-be-a-man stare. Doughnut sighed, picked up a shred of brains, and stuck it in his mouth. It was a moment of high drama, but I couldn't help glancing at Melinda to see if she was savoring it as much as I was. That's how I missed Doughnut's bolt for the bathroom. He only made it as far as the tall wastebasket beside the door. And when he let go, it was pretty awesome. The metal can resonated like a kettledrum, magnifying the heave into something truly stupendous—a barf worthy of the Doughnut in all his grossness. The sound and the smell set off a chain reaction that sent about a dozen girls and just as many guys out the door and down the hall to the rest rooms.

Mr. O'Brien stood at the front of the class, hands on hips, glaring at Doughnut's broad rear end as Doughnut heaved a couple more times. He shook his head. "Well, that's it for today, I guess." He waved a hand at the few of us who still sat frozen in our seats. "The rest of you can go. I've got to get Doughnut cleaned up. Don, Melinda, come get your dishes."

I picked up the half-empty loaf pan and followed Melinda out. At the door I paused. "I'm sorry, Mr. O'Brien."

He slapped me on the shoulder. "Not your fault we've got a bunch of sissies in this class. You did a great job. The most original ethnic dish we've ever had. An A+ all the way. Right, Doughnut?"

Doughnut leaned back on his heels, his face the color of dirty gym socks. "Right, Coach."

"As a matter of fact, we've got a big game Friday night," Mr. O'Brien went on. "Maybe I'll have Don bring a couple of pans of brains by the locker room. Some fried brains and some 'blood of the Cossacks' might be just the thing you boys need to fire up for a game against the conference champions. What do you think, Doughnut?"

Doughnut looked at Mr. O'Brien and then at me. *I am dead*, I thought. "Right, Coach. I'll do better. I promise. I'll be the first one to take some."

"Darn right you will. Now, are you man enough to take that wastebasket down to the custodian's room and wash it out?"

"Yes, sir."

We watched him trudge down the hall, head hanging.

Mr. O'Brien slapped me on the shoulder a final time. "Good work, Shadis. See you tomorrow."

A half block from the school, Melinda was sitting on one of the swings in the playground behind the grade school. "Okay," she said. "What were they really?"

"Fettuccine."

"Yeah, I thought so. Did O'Brien catch on?"

I shrugged. "Who knows? If he did, he decided to go along with the joke."

"You're lucky. You were way out on the edge. What did he say to you?"

"Not much. He said maybe he'd have me bring a couple of pans of brains to the locker room before Friday night's game."

She laughed. "Cool. I bet half those jocks would lose their lunch. Are you going to do it?"

"Are you kidding? I don't have that kind of death wish. I think pig brains may be real hard to find for the next few weeks."

"And sheep, goat, and calf brains?"

"Them, too," I said.

She laughed again. "I'm glad you did it. Took Doughnut down a notch." She grinned at me. "And put you up a couple, even if nobody knows what you really had in that pan but me."

I shrugged. "That's okay. I don't want to be a dead hero. . . . Hey, you walking my way?"

"Yeah, I could do that," she said. "Definitely."

Alden R. Carter

Like most stories, "Pig Brains" started with a real incident. My fifteen-year-old son, Brian, needed to bring a snack representing his ethnic heritage to his social studies class. Looking through his mother's Lithuanian cookbook, he found a recipe for fried brains. We didn't try to find the real item but used pasta from the beginning. The "brain dip" was a late-night inspiration when we were getting punchy. Anyway, the hoax worked. To this date most of his classmates and his teacher (we think) still believe that they ate fried brains that day. No one got sick, but two or three people did express a certain queasiness.

In writing "Pig Brains," I thought back to my own self at fifteen: short and scrawny. (Not my son, who is tall and a serious jock.) I recalled a few (large) people I disliked and put them together into the Doughnut. I sorted through all the various girls I'd had crushes on and came up with a model for Melinda. Then I wrote the story and had a great time doing it.

Brian is, of course, somewhat concerned that the publication of *On the Edge* will let the pig out of the bag. But a couple of years have passed since the day he brought "pig brains" to school, and I think his classmates will forgive him. At least I hope so.

Alden R. Carter has published more than thirty books for children and young adults. Six of his novels have been named American Library Association Best Books. In 1994 his novel *Up Country* was named to ALA's list Best of the Best: The 100 Best Young Adult Books of the Last 25 Years. Mr. Carter lives in Marshfield, Wisconsin, with his wife (the photographer Carol Shadis Carter) and their son and daughter.

"All right," the technician's voice comes over her headphones. He's in the control room, but he sounds a million miles away. "Hold very still, and we'll get started."

There's a noise like the clip-clop of horses' hooves—not real horses, but maybe a mechanical kind someone might create if he'd never heard real ones. The noise drowns out the classical music, and in losing it, Bailey realizes why she asked for it in the first place: She knew she'd never have to listen to it again. If she'd chosen Z-98, some song she liked might be ruined for her forever. She could imagine hearing an Ace of Base song six months from now and thinking, That's the song that was playing the day they found out about my brain tumor—

But if there's a tumor, will I even be alive six months from now?

Fine?

by Margaret Peterson Haddix

"Contrary to popular opinion," the MRI technician says, "this is not a torture device, it was not invented by aliens, and it does not enable us to read your thoughts."

Bailey looks doubtfully at the huge machine in front of her. She has already forgotten what MRI stands for. Does that mean there's really something wrong with her?

"Just joking," the man says. "But you wouldn't believe the questions I get. This won't be a problem for you at all unless . . . you're not claustrophobic, are you?"

"No," Bailey says. But she has to think about the question. Wearing a hospital gown, sitting in a wheelchair, she has a hard time remembering what and who she is. Bailey Smith, sophomore at Riverside High School, all-around ordinary kid.

But I won't be ordinary if that machine finds something awful in my brain. . . .

"Good," the technician is saying. "Because I have to admit, some people do go a little nutso in there." He's a short man with glasses; he seems amused that some people might not enjoy his precious machine.

61

"Bailey will be fine," Bailey's mother says firmly from behind the wheelchair.

"Mom," Bailey protests, shorthand for "Mom, you're embarrassing me," "Mom, you're bugging me," "Mom, you're driving me crazy." Bailey has said that word that way a thousand times in the past couple of years: When her mother said she shouldn't let her bra straps show. When her mother thought people went to homecoming *with dates*. When her mother asked why Bailey didn't like Hanson's music anymore. The complaint "Mom" was usually so perfect at conveying Bailey's thoughts. But it sounds all wrong in this huge, hollow room.

"Well," the technician says, "time to get this over with."

Bailey lies down on a narrow pallet sticking out of the machine like a tongue. The technician starts to pull a covering over her head, then stops.

"Almost forgot," he says. "Want to listen to the radio while you're in there?"

"Okay," Bailey says.

"What station?"

Bailey starts to say Z-98, the station everyone at school listens to, the only station Bailey ever turns on.

"Country 101?" the technician teases. "Want to hear cowboys crying in their beer?"

"No," Bailey says. She surprises herself by deciding, "Something classical."

As soon as she's in the tube, Bailey regrets her choice. All those throbbing violins, those crashing cymbals—Bailey knows next to nothing about classical music and cares about it even less. The slow, cultured voice of the announcer—"And now we'll hear Mozart's finest concerto, at least in my humble opinion"—could drive anyone crazy. Or nutso, as the technician had said.

"All right," the technician's voice comes over her headphones. He's in the control room, but he sounds a million miles away. "Hold very still, and we'll get started."

There's a noise like the clip-clop of horses' hooves—not real horses, but maybe a mechanical kind someone might create if he'd never heard real ones. The noise drowns out the classical music, and in losing it, Bailey realizes why she asked for it in the first place: She knew she'd never have to listen to it again. If she'd chosen Z-98, some song she liked might be ruined for her forever. She could imagine hearing an Ace of Base song six months from now and thinking, *That's the song that was playing the day they found out about my brain tumor—*

But if there's a tumor, will I even be alive six months from now?

Something catches in Bailey's throat and she has to swallow a cough.

Silly, she chides herself. *Nobody's said anything about a tumor.* The only real possibility the emergency room doctor mentioned, ordering all these tests, was a stroke, which was too ridiculous to think about. Old people had strokes. Bailey is only sixteen.

Maybe they'll just find out I made the whole thing up.

But she hadn't. Her arm had gone totally numb, right

there in algebra class. She hadn't been able to feel the pencil in her fingers. And she hadn't been able to see right, she hadn't been able to hear much—Mr. Vickers's raspy voice had seemed to come at her through a tunnel. Still, she might not have said anything about it if Mr. Vickers hadn't called on her to go work a problem on the board.

"I can't . . . ," she tried to say, but she couldn't seem to make her brain think the words right, she couldn't get her mouth to move. She tried to stand up but fell down instead. Mr. Vickers had Paula Klinely take her to the nurse, the nurse called her mother, and now she's in an MRI tube listening to the clip-clop of fake horses.

The clip-clopping stops and the violins come back.

"You moved," the technician says over the headphones with the same tone of exaggerated patience as the classical music announcer. "We'll have to do that one again. The less you move, the quicker we'll be done."

"I'm sorry," Bailey apologizes, though she's not sure he can hear her. If she's going to die at sixteen, she wants people to remember her as a nice person. She can imagine people giving testimonials at her funeral: *She was always so good, so kind to animals and people alike.* Her best friend, Allison, could reminisce, *And if she found a spider indoors, she was always very careful about carrying it outside instead of killing it.* She hopes Allison would remember to say that. Maybe this technician would even come to the funeral.

I never get close to the patients, he might say. *I view everyone as just another brain scan. But here was a kid who was always so gracious and noble. She knew she was dying, but she was always concerned about other people. She always asked about my family, my pets, my—*

Bailey can't think what else the technician might be impressed by her asking about. She decides he should break down in sobs at that point.

The clip-clopping starts again. Bailey concentrates on not moving. She's very glad the MRI can't read her thoughts.

When the MRI is finally done and the technician pulls her out of the tube, Bailey scans his face for some expression—of pity, maybe, or better yet, boredom.

"Well?" she says.

"What?" he asks, looking down at the controls that lower her pallet.

"What did you find?" she asks, forgetting that she is supposed to be acting like she cares more about his dog than her life.

"Oh, I'm not allowed to discuss results with patients," the technician says. "Your doctor will review everything and then talk to you."

He's less chatty now. Does that mean anything?

Bailey climbs back into the wheelchair—something else that's ridiculous, because isn't she perfectly capable of walking now? The technician pushes her out to the waiting room, where Bailey's mother is intently reading *Golf Digest*. To the best of Bailey's knowledge, Bailey's mother has never played golf in her entire life.

"Well?" Bailey's mother asks. But she directs the

question to Bailey, not the technician. "Are you all right?"

"I'm fine," Bailey insists.

Bailey's mother lays her hand on Bailey's shoulder, something she never would have done under normal circumstances. Bailey doesn't pull away.

The technician is on the phone.

"They have a room ready for you now," he reports. "An aide will be by in a few minutes to take you up there."

He leaves, and Bailey and her mother are alone.

"Do you really feel okay?" Bailey's mother asks. "You haven't had another . . . episode?"

"No. I've just got a little headache," Bailey says. But it's just the edge of a headache—nothing Bailey would mention if she weren't in the hospital. "Do I really have to stay all night?"

"That's what the doctor said. They can't schedule the other tests until tomorrow. And—" Mom stops and starts over. "Look at it as a chance to play hooky. To avoid biology class."

She smiles brightly at Bailey, and Bailey resists the urge to retort, "I'd rather dissect frogs than die." But she realizes she'd said exactly the reverse only a week ago in the school cafeteria: "I'd rather die than dissect a frog." She remembers the exact moment she spoke the words: Sunlight had been streaming in the window behind Allison, grease was congealing on the school lunch tacos, all her friends were laughing.

Oh, God, did I bring this on myself? Bailey wonders. *I didn't really mean that. God, I'll dissect a billion frogs if you want me to. If you let me live.* But she knows from TV disease-of-the-week movies that bargaining with God never works.

"Mom, what do you think is wrong with me?" Bailey asks, and is amazed that the question comes out sounding merely conversational. She wants to whimper.

Mom keeps her smile, but it seems even less genuine now.

"I'm no doctor," she says. "But I think you blacked out because you skipped lunch to do your history report. That's all."

"I had a Hershey's bar," Bailey says.

"My point exactly," Mom says, and laughs, and Bailey feels much better. Mom wouldn't dare criticize Bailey's eating habits if she thought something was really wrong.

Would she?

Bailey's room is in the main part of the hospital, not the pediatric wing, a fact that worries Bailey's mom.

"Are you sure?" she asks the aide who is skillfully maneuvering Bailey's wheelchair past several carts of dinner trays. "She's only sixteen. Don't they—"

"Listen, lady, I just go where they send me," the aide responds. He's a thin man with sallow skin and a dark braid hanging down his back. Bailey can't decide if he would have been considered cool or a scuzz in high school. Probably a scuzz if he ended up as a hospital aide. Then she decides she shouldn't think things like that, not if she wants people to remember her as a nice person.

The aide is explaining to Mom that lots of kids have

checked in lately; the pediatric wing is full. He makes it sound like a hotel everyone wants to stay at.

"But if she's not in the pediatric wing, I can't spend the night with her," Mom frets.

"Nope. Not according to what they tell me," the aide agrees.

They arrive at the door of Bailey's room. At first glance Bailey thinks the mistake is even bigger than Mom feared: She's been given a bed in a nursing home. The room is crowded with people at least a decade or two older than Bailey's own grandparents. Then Bailey realizes that only one of the old people is actually in a bed. The rest are visitors.

"Coming through," the aide says, only barely missing knocking down one man's cane and another man's walker.

"Oh, look, Aunt Mabel's got a roommate," someone says. "Won't that be nice."

But they're all looking back and forth from Bailey to her mother, obviously confused.

"She fainted," Bailey's mother announces. "She's just in for a few tests."

It's a cue for Bailey to say, once more, "Mom!" This time she keeps her mouth shut and her head down.

The old people nod and smile. One woman says, "She looks just like my granddaughter. I'm sure she'll be fine," as if the resemblance could save Bailey's life. Another woman adds, "You know those doctors. They just don't want to get sued."

As Bailey silently climbs from the chair to the bed she

sees that her mother is smiling back at the old people, but the corners of her mouth are tighter than ever.

A nurse appears and whips a curtain between Bailey's bed and the old people. The aide fades away with a strange little wave, almost a salute. That one hand gesture makes Bailey want to call after him: *Wait! What happens to most of the people you wheel around? Do they die?*

But the nurse has begun asking questions.

"I know some of these won't apply to you," she apologizes, "but it's hospital policy. . . ."

Bailey can't help giggling at "Do you wear dentures?" and "Do you have any artificial limbs?" The nurse zips through the questions without looking up, until she reaches "Do you do recreational drugs?"

"No," Bailey says. They asked that in the emergency room, too.

"Are you sure?" The nurse squints suspiciously at Bailey.

"Yes," Bailey says. "I have never done drugs." She spaces the words out, trying to sound emphatic, but it comes out all wrong. She realizes from the way the nurse is looking at her that the nurse has done drugs and is surprised to meet a teenager who hasn't.

"My daughter," Bailey's mother interjects, "has never taken anything stronger than aspirin."

It's true, and Bailey's glad it's true, but she wants to sink through the floor with humiliation at her mother's words.

How can she care about humiliation at a time like this?

• • •

Someone comes and takes ten vials of blood from Bailey's arm. Someone else starts what he calls an IV port on the back of Bailey's left hand. It's basically a needle taped into her vein, ready for any injection she might need. Someone else takes her blood pressure and makes Bailey push on his hands with her feet, then close her eyes and hold her arms out straight.

"Good," the man says when Bailey opens her eyes.

I did that right? So I'm okay? Bailey wants to ask. But something about lying in a hospital bed has made Bailey mute. She can barely say a word to her own mother, sitting two feet away.

"Visiting hours are over," the man tells Mom in a flat voice.

"But my daughter—," Mom protests, and stops, swallows hard. Bailey is stunned. Mom is never at a loss for words. "She's only sixteen, and—"

"No visitors after five. Hospital policy," the man says, but there's a hint of compassion in his voice now. "We'll take good care of her. I promise."

"Well . . ." Still Mom hesitates. She looks at Bailey. "I know the Montinis didn't really want to take Andrew overnight, they were just being nice, and with your dad away . . ."

Andrew is Bailey's younger brother, seven years old and, everyone agrees, a pure terror. Bailey's dad is away on a business trip. Mom couldn't even reach him on the phone from the emergency room. Bailey can't see why Mom is telling her what she already knows. Then Bailey understands: Mom is asking Bailey for permission to leave.

They're going to make you leave anyway, Bailey wants to say. *What do you want me to do?* But it's strange. For a minute Bailey feels like she's the mother and her mother is the daughter.

"Go on," she says magnanimously. "I'll be fine."

But as soon as her mother is out the door, Bailey wants to run after her, crying, "Mom-mee! Don't go!" just like she used to do at preschool, years and years and years ago.

Once they're alone together, Bailey's roommate, Mabel, gets gabby.

"Ten days I've been lying in this hospital bed," she announces, speaking to the TV as much as to Bailey. "First they say it's my kidneys, then it's my bladder—or is that the same thing? I forget. Then there's my spleen—"

Bailey can't imagine lying in any hospital bed for ten days. She's already antsy, after just two hours. The sheets are suffocating her legs. She hated that spring in junior high when she signed up for track and Mom made her finish the whole season. But now she longs to run and run and run, sprints and relays and maybe even marathons.

I've never run a marathon. What else will I never get to do if I die now?

Bailey is glad when Mabel distracts her by announcing joyfully, "Oh good, dinner."

An aide slides a covered tray in front of Mabel and one in front of Bailey.

"We didn't know what you wanted, 'cause you weren't here last night," the aide says accusingly.

Bailey lifts the cover. Dinner is some kind of meat covered in brown gravy, green beans blanched to a sickly gray, mashed potatoes that could pass for glue, gummy apples with a slab of soggy pie dough on top—food Bailey would never eat in a million years. And yet, somehow, she finds that she can eat it, and does, every bite.

See? she wants to tell someone. *I'm healthy. So healthy I can eat this slop and not die.*

Beside her tray is a menu for the next day. Bailey studies it as carefully as a cram sheet for some major final exam. Hospital Food 101, maybe. If she were still here for dinner tomorrow night, she'd have a choice of meat loaf or fried chicken, chocolate cake or ice cream.

But of course she won't be here tomorrow night. Because they're going to find out, first thing tomorrow, that there's nothing wrong with her.

She hopes.

The aide comes back for Bailey's tray.

"You didn't fill that out," she says, pointing at Bailey's menu.

"I'm just here overnight. I don't need to—," Bailey protests.

"Fill it out anyway," the aide orders.

Meekly, Bailey puts check marks in little boxes. Pancakes for breakfast. Chicken salad for lunch. Meat loaf and chocolate cake.

It doesn't matter. If she's still here tomorrow night, she knows, she won't be hungry.

The aide glances out Bailey's window. "Man, look at that traffic," she moans.

Bailey looks up, puzzled, and the aide has to explain: "Rush hour."

It's five forty-five. Bailey is stunned that the rest of the world is going on outside this hospital room. She is stunned to realize that she should be at marching band practice, right now, with Mr. Chaynowski ordering them to do a final run-through of "Another Opening, Another Show," before marching back to the school, packing up her clarinet, joking with her friends.

It's too weird to think about. She's actually glad when Mabel flips on the local news.

Three hours later Bailey is ready to scream. She can't stand the TV. It's into sitcoms now, old-lady ones Bailey never watches. Bailey has never noticed before, but on TV everyone smiles all the time. Everyone laughs at everything.

How dare they?

Searching desperately for something to distract her, Bailey notices her backpack, cast off in the corner. She pulls out her algebra book.

She is a normal sixteen-year-old. Sixteen-year-olds do homework on Tuesday nights.

Bailey missed the end of class, when Mr. Vickers assigns the homework, but he always assigns the odd problems. She takes out a pencil and paper, and imagines what Mr. Vickers will say on Thursday: *Bailey, good to have you back. Remember to make up the homework.*

Bailey will use her airiest voice: *Oh, it's already done. Here.*

And he'll stare in amazement.

Why, Bailey, he'll say, admiration creeping into his voice. *You're such a conscientious student.*

Mr. Vickers is straight out of college, and a real hottie. Lots of girls have crushes on him.

Why, there you were on the verge of death, he might say. *And you still—*

Bailey doesn't want to think anymore about what Mr. Vickers might say. The numbers swim in front of her eyes.

The phone rings. Mabel answers it and grunts disappointedly, "It's for you."

Bailey picks up her phone.

"Oh, Bay-ley!" It's Allison.

Bailey is suddenly so happy she can't speak. She grins as widely as someone on TV.

"Bailey?" Allison asks. "Are you all right?"

"I'm fine," Bailey says. But she's not happy anymore. Allison's voice is all wrong, and so is Bailey's. She can't seem to make her words come out right.

"Well," Allison says, and stops. It strikes Bailey that Allison doesn't know what to say either. Allison—who usually talks so much she could get a speeding ticket for her mouth.

"What'd you think? That I was going to be the dead person in the yearbook for our class?" Bailey jokes desperately. Their yearbook came out last week, and Allison had gone on and on about how every year the senior class had someone die, usually in a car wreck, and that person got a whole page of the yearbook dedicated to him. Last year the dead person was the head cheerleader, so there were lots of pictures. Allison and Bailey and their friends had spent an entire lunch period imagining what a memorial page might say for everyone in their class.

"Imogene Rogers, world's biggest airhead, floated off into outer space . . . John Vhymes, biggest show-off, thought he had a better idea for running heaven than God does . . . Stanley Witherspoon, died two years ago but nobody noticed until now . . ."

It had been funny last week. It isn't now. Bailey hears Allison inhale sharply. Bailey tries to pretend she didn't say anything.

"So what happened after I left?" Bailey asks. "Anything good?"

"Everyone was just talking about you," Allison says. "Do you know what's wrong yet?"

Suddenly Bailey can't talk to Allison. She just can't.

"Listen, Al, some nurse is coming in in a minute to take my blood pressure. I'll call you later, okay?"

It isn't really a lie. They're always coming in to take her blood pressure.

Allison hangs up. Bailey hopes Mabel's hearing is as bad as her kidneys.

Bailey is surprised that she can fall asleep. She's even more surprised when they wake her up at 6 A.M. for an electro-cardiogram.

"But my mom—," she protests groggily.

"They don't want to test your mom's heart," the aide says. "They want to test yours."

Bailey is climbing into the wheelchair when the phone rings.

"Oh, Bailey," her mother's voice rushes at her. "They said you were already up. I was just getting ready to come down there, but something awful happened—the car won't start. I called Triple A, but it's going to be an hour before they get out here. I'm looking for someone to give me a ride or loan me a car. . . . I am so sorry. This is incredibly bad timing. Are you okay?"

It's easiest for Bailey to say automatically, like a robot, "I'm fine."

"I'll get there as soon as I can," Mom assures her.

"I know. That's fine," Bailey says. But the words have no meaning anymore.

Down in the EKG room they put cold gel on Bailey's chest and the technician runs a probe along Bailey's rib cage. Even though the technician is a woman, Bailey is embarrassed because the probe keeps running into her breasts.

"Um-hmm," the technician mutters to herself.

Bailey knows better now than to ask what the "Um-hmm" means. She can't see the TV screen the technician peers into. The technician pushes harder and harder on the probe, until it feels like an animal trying to burrow between Bailey's ribs. Bailey can't help crying out.

The technician looks up, surprised, as if she'd forgotten that Bailey is an actual human being, capable of feeling pain.

"Sorry," she says, and pushes the probe down even harder.

I am just a body here, Bailey thinks. *Nobody here knows or cares that I'm nice to animals and small children, that I do my homework on time. That I'm a person.* She wants to say something to make the technician really see her, but the longer Bailey lies on the cold table in her hospital gown, the more she feels like all her personality is leaching away. She is just a body.

Is that what it's like to die?

Another technician in another room repeats the procedure—the cold gel, the hard probe—on Bailey's neck and shoulders, checking out the blood vessels that lead to her brain.

This woman talks constantly—about her kids, her garden, her diet—but it's not like she's really talking to Bailey. Even when the woman asks a direct question, "Have you ever heard of a geranium growing like that?" the woman doesn't stop long enough for Bailey to answer.

Bailey is crying, and the woman doesn't even notice.

Bailey thinks she'll have to dry her tears and wipe her eyes before she sees her mother. She can't wait to see her mother. She wants Mom to think about all these horrible things so Bailey doesn't have to. She wants Mom there to remember what Bailey is really like, so Bailey can remember how to act normal.

But when Bailey gets back to her room, there's only a message. Mom's stuck in traffic.

Mom left the number for the Montinis' car phone,

but Bailey doesn't call it. She turns her head to the wall so her roommate won't see, and lies in bed sobbing silently. She's not sure if she's crying about the stalled traffic or the painful probe or the shame of having made jokes about dead people in the yearbook. Or the fact that whatever made Bailey faint yesterday might also make her die. *It really could happen,* Bailey thinks. *People die of terrible diseases all the time. There's no reason that it shouldn't happen to me.*

For the first time Bailey realizes none of her fears have been real before. When she imagined the MRI technician speaking at her funeral, the memorial page in the yearbook, Mr. Vickers's response to her devotion to algebra, even her personality leaching away, it was just a fantasy to her. Role-playing. A game.

But Bailey is standing on the edge of something awful, balanced between two possible futures. On one side is the life she's always known: homework and marching band and jokes with Allison and groans at her mother. Health. A future just like her past. And on the other side, over the cliff into whatever her illness is, is more time in hospital beds, more technicians seeing her innards but not really seeing her, more time crying alone. And maybe—death. Bailey longs fervently for her normal life back. In her mind it positively glows, an utterly joyous existence. Ordinary never looked so good.

But it's not her choice which future she gets.

"Hello?" someone calls tentatively.

Bailey pauses to hide the evidence of her crying before she turns. But, strangely, she's not crying anymore.

A man pulls the curtain around her bed, to give some privacy from her roommate.

"I'm Dr. Rogers, your neurologist," he says. "I've looked at all your test results, and—"

Bailey's heart pounds. She can barely hear him for the surge of blood in her ears. She feels dizzier than she felt yesterday, when everyone said she fainted.

"Shouldn't my mom be here to hear this?" Bailey asks. "She's coming soon."

Dr. Rogers looks at his watch.

"No. I can't wait."

He's treating me like I'm a grown-up, Bailey marvels. But the thought has an echo: *Grown-up enough to die.*

"This is a classic case," Dr. Rogers is saying. "I'm surprised nobody caught it yesterday. They still would have wanted the tests, just to be sure. . . . What you had was a migraine headache."

A headache? Not a stroke? Not a tumor? As soon as Dr. Rogers has said the inoffensive word, all the possibilities Bailey feared instantly recede. She's a million miles away from that frightening cliff now. Of course she isn't going to die. How silly she'd been, to think she might. How silly, to think he'd tell her she was dying without her mother there.

Dr. Rogers is still talking, about the link between chocolate and migraines, about how common migraines are for young girls, about how it was perfectly normal for Bailey to get the symptoms of a migraine headache before her head even began to hurt. But Bailey barely listens. She's thinking about getting her ordinary life back—ordinary life with maybe a headache every now and then.

Fine? **79**

Bailey doesn't care—her head barely even hurt yesterday. She doesn't expect a mere headache to change anything at all. She waits for the glow to fade from her view of her ordinary life, and it does, but not entirely. Even with headaches she has a pretty good life.

Bailey's mother rushes into the room just then, apologizing right and left.

"Doctor, you must think I'm a terrible mother, not to be here at a time like this. What did you find out? Please tell me—it was just a fluke, right?"

"Mom," Bailey protests, in humiliation, with perfect emphasis.

The complaint never sounded so wonderful before.

Margaret Peterson Haddix

When my son was barely three months old, he choked on his own phlegm and stopped breathing. Though he went without air for only a matter of seconds, it felt like an eternity. Horrified, I rushed him to the doctor, wanting mostly to be assured that such a thing would never happen again. Instead, my baby was admitted to the hospital for observation and testing. For the next twenty-four hours, trapped in his hospital room, I alternated between terror and boredom. I felt like begging the doctor to keep my son hooked to monitors for the rest of his life. But I also had to fight the urge to rip all the wires and sensors off my fat, innocent, healthy-looking baby and rush him out of that nightmarish place once and for all. This instinct, it turned out, was the most reasonable—he was absolutely fine.

Three years later it was my turn to be admitted to a hospital because of a disturbing episode in the midst of otherwise good health. Like Bailey in "Fine?" I was diagnosed with a migraine headache after being tested for many worse possibilities. (I realize that migraines are a horrendous problem for many people, but for me it was just a strange, almost painless occurrence.)

So I've been fortunate that most of my hospital visits have had happy endings. Hovering over each experience, though, has been the knowledge that not everyone gets good news at the end.

As a writer, I don't do well leaving intense real-life experiences alone. They nag at my consciousness until I get them down on paper. But they are almost always changed somehow in the process, fictionalized by the questions I ask myself along the way. I wondered what it would be like to go through something like my son's hospitalization if he had been old enough to understand what was going on. What would it be like, say, to be the mother of a teenager in the hospital for tests? In the case of my own hospitalization, the thing that bothered me most when I thought about fatal diseases was the possibility that I might not get to see my kids grow up. What if I'd been worried about getting a chance to grow up myself?

Margaret Peterson Haddix has worked as a newspaper reporter in Indianapolis, and as a community college instructor in Danville, Illinois. She and her family now live in Columbus, Ohio.

Several of Ms. Haddix's books have been named American Library Association Best Books for Young Adults. Her first book, *Running Out of Time*, was also an Edgar Award nominee, a Junior Library Guild Selection, and a Readers Choice Award winner in Arizona, Oklahoma, and Maryland. Her second book, *Don't You Dare Read This, Mrs. Dunphrey*, won the International Reading Association Children's Book Award. Her other books include *Leaving Fishers, Among the Hidden, Just Ella*, and the forthcoming *Turnabout*.

I am walking down the hall in the south wing when suddenly you are there in front of me, going the opposite way. We are going to collide, I think. Our eyes meet for a nanosecond—I can almost taste the root beer—then they skitter off me like water hitting a hot griddle and your body turns slightly and you slide past as if I were no more than a patch of thick air.

My heart is banging with rib-cracking ferocity. I clap a hand to my zit to see if it has exploded, but find only a hot lump of potential. Did you see it? No. You saw nothing. Not my zit.

Not me.

I do not exist in your world. Not yet.

But I will.

Hot Lava

by Pete Hautman

I wake up with a sort of tingling sensation in my face at the exact point where my left nostril, my cheek, and my upper lip come together. I reach up to touch it. The spot is tender, but I can't feel a bump or anything with my finger. I get up and look in the mirror. The disaster area is faintly pink, but not like you'd notice it if you didn't know where to look. Not yet.

A subterranean. A troglodyte.

I eat my cornflakes and I think about your eyes, the exact color of the sun seen through root beer candy. I think how your perfect nose touches your perfect cheek, blemish free. I think these things as I tie my shoes, as the tingling in my face becomes a faint throb. Is it getting redder?

Vesuvius, Paricutín, Krakatoa.

I brush my teeth, imagining the curl of your lip, your sharp look of disgust as you recoil from the sight of my eruption. Passing me in the hall, notebook gripped lightly in your long fingers, your root beer eyes sliding across my anonymous features, snagging on my growing, throbbing volcano.

I could skip school. Hide in the woods and eat berries and drink swamp water until it subsides. Protect you from its ugliness.

I touch it lightly with the handle of my toothbrush. The swelling has begun.

There are three types of volcanoes.

Shield volcanoes are seeping, oozing, swelling sores on the earth's surface, like hives, or an infected cut. They build up layer after layer of hot, hardened planet juice. They are quiet and forceful, like my father. There is a mountain on Mars called Olympus Mons, a dead shield volcano 15 miles high. Who measured it? No one will say.

I could cover it with a Band-Aid, but the location is awkward and people would ask me why I had a Band-Aid on the place where my nostril meets my cheek meets my upper lip. I could lie or I could tell them the truth. Both would be unbearable. Besides, if everyone put tape on their zits, we'd look like a school full of mummies.

The second type of eruption is called a cinder cone volcano. One day in 1943 a farmer in Mexico saw some smoke coming from a crack in his cornfield. Pretty soon the crack was coughing out hot ash and glowing cinders. The next morning a smoldering, spitting, spewing thirty-five-foot-high pile of ash covered part of his field, and it was still growing. Today, Paricutín is more than 1000 feet high, an ugly gray Earth zit.

We have been studying volcanoes in geology, a class filled with lots of smart, pimply kids. While I am studying rocks and dirt, you are playing soccer. I can feel the vibrations of your feet pounding the planet's crust.

Earth is a ball of hot pudding with a dried-out, cracked surface. Islands of crust floating on a gelatinous pudding sea. Crustal plates grinding their ragged edges together, and where they meet, a seep of chocolate. Volcanoes love these seams, these fault lines. And where plates come together—nostril, cheek, lip—there is fire.

Mount Saint Helens, Mount Fuji, Mount Pinatubo.

The biggest and most dramatic volcanoes are called stratovolcanoes. They do it all. They spew ash and ooze lava and when things get really tense they can explode like Mount Saint Helens or my mother.

She says, "You should drink your milk."

"I just brushed my teeth."

"You are wasting food," she says.

I search her face for signs of imminent eruption, but see only tiredness. This morning my mother is dormant. She will not throw a fit over a half glass of milk. She will sigh and pour it down the sink, or maybe use it on her own bowl of cornflakes.

"You look nice," she tells me.

Kiss of death. I go back to my room and change my shirt.

I have three ways to get to school.

I can walk the 1.2 miles directly, or I can walk .6 miles in the other direction and catch the Number 26 bus, or I can walk 2.1 miles to the east and catch the Number 13 bus. Why would I do that, you ask? Because it is *your* bus. But on this morning I do not want you to see me with my face ready to explode. Later, with one hand in front of my face, I will pass you in the hall, inhaling as we reach maximum proximity.

I load my books into my backpack, an old canvas Boy Scout model that used to be my dad's. Everybody gives me crap about it but I think it's cool. I look again in the mirror. Vesuvius is rumbling. Volcanologists predict an eruption by lunch.

I'm walking toward the front door, still considering my transportation options, when I get stuck. I imagine your face, and it comes to me with such intense, high-definition clarity that I stop in my tracks and close my eyes. I can see the shape of your lips, and the way your thick black hair falls, casting a shadow across your blemish-free forehead. I can count your eyelashes. I can hear you breathing.

"Chris!" My mother's voice, like the crack of a whip. Your image blinks out.

"What?"

"What are you doing? You'll miss your bus!"

"I'll walk."

"You'll be late." Her face swims into view, eyebrows frowning. "Are you all right?"

"I'm fine."

"You were just standing in the middle of the room with your eyes closed."

"I was thinking."

"You can't think and walk at the same time?"

I start moving toward the door. "I'm going, I'm going."

She watches me. I feel her eyes as I reach the sidewalk. Left, toward the school . . . or right, in the direction of the bus stop?

I turn left. I need the walking time. I hear my mother shout after me—she knows I'll be late again—and I break into a jog. I run until I am out of sight, then slow to a foot-dragging shamble. First hour is trigonometry. I don't need trig. I need a zit doctor.

I keep thinking about volcanoes.

Krakatoa is a volcanic island in the Indian Ocean. In 1883 Krakatoa started grumbling and muttering to itself. The natives became restless. Most of them got into their boats and left. Good thing. Krakatoa, a stratovolcano, blew its top, making the loudest sound in recorded history. People heard the blast 2000 miles away. Two-thirds of the island was blown to cinders and dust.

I am running again, trying to blow off some pressure. I get to school at the same time as the Number 13 bus. Panting and wheezing, I watch the bus unload.

There you are, coming off the bus, chatting with your friends, going up the wide, shallow steps and into the foyer. I follow, staying back far enough so that my zit won't blind you. I follow you to your history class. I watch you enter the classroom, then slip on past. I take my seat in Mr. Nguyen's trigonometry class a few seconds before the bell. Mr. Nguyen is already scrawling numbers on the board.

My friend Pat Holcroft leans over and says, "What's that thing on your nose?"

"Krakatoa," I say. "Shut up."

Pat laughs. The bell rings.

On the way from trig to geology I am thinking too hard about Krakatoa and not paying attention to where I'm going. I am walking down the hall in the south wing when suddenly you are there in front of me, going the opposite way. We are going to collide, I think. Our eyes meet for a nanosecond—I can almost taste the root beer—then they skitter off me like water hitting a hot griddle and your body turns slightly and you slide past as if I were no more than a patch of thick air.

My heart is banging with rib-cracking ferocity. I clap a hand to my zit to see if it has exploded, but find only a hot lump of potential. Did you see it? No. You saw nothing. Not my zit.

Not me.

I do not exist in your world. Not yet.

But I will.

I take my seat in geology class. Rock samples line the window sills: igneous, sedimentary, metamorphic. I can see the soccer field and, beyond, a range of low hills. Ancient volcanoes? Perhaps. Perhaps it is time for desperate measures, I think. I think of the things I will do.

I will stand up on my chair in Mrs. Jackson's English class and declare my love for the way you hold your notebook. I will shout out my appreciation for each of your root beer eyes. I will scream adorations until they drag me away, and you will feel the power of my love and you will follow me.

I will fall to my hands and knees before you in the hallway and shower your feet with kisses. My lips will devour you, and you will take my head in your hands and draw me to you and we will be Velcro together.

I will buy a hundred cans of red spray paint and I will write a thousand passionate words on the walls of the school in letters ten feet high, your name and my name, again and again, until they tear the paint from my grasp. You will think of me as they sandblast the walls. I will dedicate the sandblasting to you.

I will chain myself to the dish on top of the school and I will send my feelings skyward. My love for you will strike the satellite and be broadcast into living rooms in every corner of the planet. You will hear me through asphalt shingles, I will echo through your bones.

Mr. Balto is writing something on the board. I open my notebook and copy down the words: *geothermal energy*. I look out the window and see the soccer players running out onto the field. Which one are you?

I will drill a hole in the very center of the soccer field—a mile, a hundred miles deep until I strike magma.

I will ride the hot lava back up through the crust. All that I feel for you, all that is surging and bubbling and heaving inside of me will burst forth. The volcanic cone will grow, soon to cover the athletic fields, and then the school, and then the city, and it will be named for you and me.

I will do all these things and more to make you notice me.

But I will not do them today.

Pete Hautman

People ask how I can write stories about and for teenagers when I don't have any children. I usually say, "I used to be one." I have a theory about parents: Some of them, as soon as they have one, forget what it was like to be a kid.

One day I was remembering some of the really stupid things I did when I was a teenager. Sometimes I got caught, sometimes I was horribly embarrassed, and a few times I got hurt—but mostly I had a lot of close calls. The scariest stuff, though, was the stuff I thought about doing but decided not to: the bridge I didn't jump off, the train I didn't hop, the pill I didn't take.

"Hot Lava" is a story about volcanoes, love, acne, and the things we decide not to do.

Pete Hautman lives in Tucson, Arizona, in the winter, and the town of Stockholm, Wisconsin, in the summer. He lives with mystery writer Mary Logue.

Mr. Hautman's first YA novel, *Mr. Was,* was listed as an American Library Association Best Book, named Young Adult Book of the Year by the Michigan Library Association, and nominated for an Edgar Award by the Mystery Writers of America.

His latest novel, *Stone Cold,* is about a teenage boy who develops a taste and a talent for high-stakes poker.

Dad ran past me too. Eric turned, his back pressed against the door, and Dad slowed, began approaching him the way you would a frightened animal. "It's okay, Eric. Just take it easy. Everything's going to be okay."

Mom had also slipped by me. "Eric, please let us help you."

Eric's eyes widened. He bent low and charged under their arms. He ran for Mom's chopping knife, which was lying out on the cutting board surrounded by chunks of vegetables. It was a good foot long. He held it point out in front of him. "Don't come near me," he said.

Secret Numbers

by Winifred Morris

Eric had already missed three days of work when I brought Tyler to the house.

I was working that summer too, at a day camp. That was where I'd met Tyler. We were the only sixteen-year-old counselors at the camp, and I was beginning to hope we'd become more than friends. So when I discovered he liked Rockabilly, I told him about the chat room Eric had helped me find.

Tyler couldn't believe it. "People talk about Rockabilly on the Internet? I thought I was the only one who liked that stuff," he said.

So after all the moms had picked up their kids that day, and all the sticky collages had been put away, I drove Tyler to my house.

But the computer refused to cooperate. Here I was, shoulder-to-shoulder with this guy, and all I could get on the screen were scary messages about "illegal operations." Every time I got close to the chat room I'd promised, we were kicked off the Internet. Tyler tried to be helpful, but you could tell he knew less than me.

"This is clearly a job for Eric," I finally said. "In fact, it's probably his fault."

"Your brother?"

"I know, looking at me, you'd never guess it, but my brother is smart. And he tries to keep this old PC on the cutting edge. No telling what he's done to it. I'll get him."

But Tyler didn't wait there. He followed me up the stairs. And right away I could feel myself wishing he hadn't, even though I couldn't have told anyone why. Eric was sometimes shy around people he didn't know, but solving computer problems, that was what he loved. It was what he was majoring in. It was what he did at his summer job.

But he hadn't gone to that job for the last three days. Because he was sick. Or something.

I called, "Hey, Ear-ache, you messed up the computer again."

He didn't call back, so I kept trudging up the stairs. I got to the door of his room, with Tyler right behind me. Eric just lay on his bed staring up at the ceiling. I said, "What did you do to it this time? All I get are error messages."

It took a while for his eyes to shift down to me. Then they slid across my face too quick, and he still didn't say anything.

Which made me say, "Are you really sick?" It seemed a dumb question. Why else would he stay home? But he didn't seem to have the flu. He hadn't even *said* he was sick. In the mornings he'd get up and get dressed as if he were going to work. Then he'd just go back to his room instead.

"It's okay," said Tyler. "We can try it some other time, can't we? I mean, this isn't my only chance to come over, is it, Kristen?"

"No, of course not." And I returned Tyler's smile, tried to act like nothing strange was going on. "The problem could be on the Internet. Sometimes it gets messed up."

But then Eric said in this quiet, flat voice that made it even creepier, "Get away from her. Get away."

I yelled at him, "What's wrong with you? You really *are* an ear-ache!" But Tyler was all the way down the stairs by then.

I chased after him, and I tried to explain it away. Maybe Eric was stressed out by his job. He was so good at this computer stuff, he was doing work that was usually done by people much older. Or maybe he was worried about his senior year of college that was coming up. He was going to be taking some very tough classes. "The guy just pushes himself too hard. It's got him depressed or something."

Tyler said he needed to get home. He wouldn't even let me drive him there. He tried to claim he *liked* riding the bus.

"How could Eric do that to me?" I yelled at Mom as I ran past the kitchen. I slammed my way into my room, wishing I could turn back the clock. And this time I wouldn't bring Tyler home, or I wouldn't ask Eric to help me, or I'd tell Tyler to wait downstairs. I came up with a million ways to prevent that awful moment.

Right then I thought it was the worst moment of my life.

• • •

I can do so little to help. At least I did what I could. I saw he wasn't what he seemed. Maybe she wasn't either. Maybe none of us are.

But she looked so much like Kristen, I tried to protect her from him.

Mom didn't do church, but she did dinner with almost the same kind of faith. She believed as long as we all ate dinner together—I had to have a school function or an invitation to someone's house to get out of it—none of the bad things you hear about on the news would be able to touch our family.

So she made me come out of my room and sit there across from Eric, him acting as if nothing had happened. And sick? Before I'd finished my salad, he'd wolfed down a plate of spaghetti just as fast as he ever did and was helping himself to more.

I was about to tell him what a jerk he was when Dad said, "Eric, how are you feeling?"

Eric stopped eating but didn't even look up. He really was being a jerk.

Dad shoved his half-full plate aside. "Well, I talked to Jim again—your boss. But I don't feel right about this. They have deadlines to meet. They're counting on you. If tomorrow you still don't feel like going to work, we'd like you to see a doctor."

"Why won't you tell us what's wrong?" said Mom, and she did one of her Mom-reaches. She did that sort of thing all the time, just touched your shoulder, or straightened your collar, or brushed back your hair.

But Eric pulled away.

She jumped up and carried her plate to the sink. She stood there running tons of water over that plate.

"Well, we don't have to decide tonight," said Dad. "We'll see how you feel in the morning."

Eric went back to eating spaghetti.

The doctor can't change what's happening. They're everywhere now.

But I let him touch me. I didn't care about him.

And it turned out he was one of the shielded ones. Some people are. I feel them brush against me when I haven't had a chance to move away, and it doesn't leap across to them. They keep on walking, unscarred.

Maybe I have some control over the way it moves through me. I haven't been told everything yet.

The next evening Eric's girlfriend called. She asked, "How's Eric?"

I had no idea what to say.

She said, "Last time I talked to him, he sounded really strange. And he hasn't called me since. Do you think he's mad at me?"

Right then I wished Lennie weren't so easy to make friends with. I said, "How should I know?"

"So he hasn't said anything about me?"

"He hasn't said much of anything about anything. Look, don't you want to talk to *him*?"

"Sure, I just thought . . . I'm sorry, Kristen. . . ."

I left the phone hanging from the kitchen wall, her apologies still sputtering out, and yelled up the stairs, "Hey, Ear-ache, Lennie's on the phone."

No response.

I yelled again. Still not a word. But I could hear him moving up there, so I gave him as much time as I could. If he didn't come, what would I tell her? He was in the john? He'd call her back? Would he call her back?

Why was it *my* job to tell her Eric had gone weird?

I was about to give her some excuse when he appeared at the foot of the stairs. He said, "Don't."

"Don't what?"

"We have to tell everyone to be very careful now."

I held the phone out to him. "Look, it's Lennie. *You* tell her to be careful."

But he didn't take the phone. Even though he must've heard her voice. She was calling both our names.

In fact, he backed away from it as if it might be dangerous. Behind him, Mom and Dad came out of their bedroom, where they'd been ever since the doctor had called an hour ago. Eric glanced over his shoulder and shied away from them too.

He kept looking at me, at them, at me, back and forth, as they came toward him. He looked . . . squeezed. Or trapped. I said, "Lennie, I can't talk right now," and hung up just as he darted past me to the back door.

Dad ran past me too. Eric turned, his back pressed against the door, and Dad slowed, began approaching him the way you would a frightened animal. "It's okay, Eric. Just take it easy. Everything's going to be okay."

Mom had also slipped by me. "Eric, please let us help you."

Eric's eyes widened. He bent low and charged under their arms. He ran for Mom's chopping knife, which was lying out on the cutting board surrounded by chunks of vegetables. It was a good foot long. He held it point out in front of him. "Don't come near me," he said.

"Eric!" screamed Mom. "What are you doing? Put that down!"

Dad just turned and came toward him again in that same quiet way. "Stay back," he said to me and Mom, and to Eric he kept crooning that stuff about things being okay.

Mom said, "Dennis, you be careful too. Eric, please put that down." Then, "What's going on?"

Eric made another charge, past me again, now out of the kitchen. He was heading for the front door, but I saw him stop and turn there too, as if the doors of the house were barriers he couldn't cross. Dad raced after him, telling me and Mom to stay where we were. Mom grabbed me in her arms. I clung to her. What *was* going on?

Then, in something like slow motion, while Eric stood backed up against the front door, the knife still thrust out in front of him, and Dad still crooning at him, she picked up the phone and dialed 911.

It's their plan to use me, but I succeeded. I didn't let it touch anyone.

Except the ones who came.

And they wore visible shields.

What had happened to Eric? That was all I could think about as the days went by and Eric didn't come home. But I told myself he was going to be all right. That job must've been too much for him, but now he was in a hospital, so he'd get well soon.

Whenever Mom or Dad tried to tell me something else, their voices breaking over the words, I refused to listen.

Then one day Tyler said, "How's your crazy brother? Has he got your computer working yet?"

I felt this twisting in my stomach. Shame? Fear? I grabbed a soccer ball and pretended I hadn't heard.

But that evening I turned the computer on for the first time since Eric had been taken away. I stared at the screen, with error messages stopping me no matter what I tried to do, and I saw Eric again, strapped down to the gurney as they rolled him into the ambulance, his eyes focused far away.

His brain stopping him because it had quit working right.

I fought with that computer until the screen was just a blur of tears. By then I had it so messed up it might never work again.

The next day, as soon as I got to the camp, before any of the little kids had arrived, I said to Tyler, "My brother has schizophrenia. It isn't funny."

The kids liked Tyler for the way he took everything with an easy grin. I had too. But now it was a relief to see that grin disappear. "I'm sorry. I didn't know."

"How could you? None of us knew."

"But why? Is it the computer thing? I mean, people who are into that are sometimes kind of weird."

"No, it has nothing to do with that. Nobody knows why it happens. Sometimes it just does."

The kids started showing up then, which was good. I didn't want to explain any more. But I was glad I'd told him. Even though I still didn't believe it myself.

I'd done it for Eric.

It was my way of making up for how angry I'd been at him.

I guess I'd started listening to Mom and Dad by then. But I was still picking through the things they said. Mostly what I heard was that Eric was responding well to his medication. And the next week, when I found him sitting at the computer again, flicking the keys and the mouse just the way he always had—so fast, so sure of himself—I felt I'd been right. All those other things they'd told me couldn't be true.

Eric hit a few more keys and said, "I think it's fixed."

I sat down in the other chair. "Thanks. I'm glad you're home."

But he didn't answer me.

And he would have, before.

I said, "I've been trying to fix that computer."

He spun his chair toward me. But his eyes avoided me. And his face was like a wall.

Whatever was inside him was completely hidden.

I said, "It was really hot today. All the kids wanted to do was swim," the words sounding stupid, more the kind of thing you'd say to a stranger. But now I saw he was still strange.

His eyes stayed fixed on the floor somewhere between the two of us and slightly to the side.

"You should've seen this one kid, Geoffrey. He can really dive."

Eric said, "I'm sorry I scared your friend."

That took me completely by surprise. "It's okay," I said.

"I was very sick then."

I nodded, stunned.

He raised his head, and I could feel relief easing through me. I said, "Maybe I'll invite him over again. He understands what happened." Eric, finally, looked me in the eye.

But what he said was, "Do you know the secret numbers?"

The relief turned cold in my chest. "No, I don't know any secret numbers. I wish I did."

He shrugged, and his eyes slipped back to the floor. He was silent again. Still hidden.

Now I was silent too.

Until I thought to say, "Mom's made her sausage pie. It smelled really good when I passed through the kitchen."

That got him to look up at me again. He even smiled a wry smile. "Well, you know how Mom is about dinner. Guess we'd better go eat it." Right then he was just the way he'd always been.

"Yeah, guess we'd better," I said, and went to the kitchen with him.

Winifred Morris

This is a very personal story for me. My brother has suffered from schizophrenia for more than thirty years. Unfortunately, back in 1965 when he was first struck with it, schizophrenia wasn't understood very well. So, unlike Kristen, I was told nothing about it. And not understanding this disease of the brain makes it even worse.

It is an extremely debilitating disease that usually strikes people when they're still young, teenagers or young adults, and it can last for many years, often a lifetime. It affects the way a person thinks and feels, but its causes are biological. We now know it isn't caused by bad parenting or personal weakness. The causes, however, are not fully known. And even though medications now allow most sufferers to lead better lives than they could before, there is still no cure.

I'm the author of four novels and five picture books, and I feel what I've been trying to do with all my writing is to explore how we deal with the difficult parts of life. Some people are beaten down. Some rise to perform amazing feats. And then there's all the rest of us.

When I wrote *Liar*, my most recent novel, which was an American Library Association Quick Pick for Reluctant Young Adult Readers, I was thinking about those kids who don't get to have loving, caring moms. Alex's mother is dishonest and sometimes abusive, just too caught up in her own weakness to give much to him. I wanted to see if Alex could, given a chance, just one very slim chance, pull away from the self-destructive patterns he'd learned from her and make a better life for himself.

Life is often difficult. What I hope to do with my writing is to celebrate the way those of us who aren't heroes still often find we have more strength than we thought.

Sara jumped in. "I've been thinking about something." She smiled. "I want to tell you about it. It means a lot to me for you to be behind me."

They didn't see it coming. They just waited, no foreboding on their faces. But I knew trouble was on the way. I didn't know what it was going to be, but I thought, Look out! I don't know who I was warning. Me, probably.

Pluto

by Gail Carson Levine

While my heart bounced from my knees to my throat and back again, Mr. Silverberry read the list of cast members. Finally he said, "The part of Lavinia will be played by . . ."

It was the weirdest thing. As he began the sentence, I went into a daydream. I imagined walking to the subway with my best friend, Alicia, and explaining that I didn't get the part because I wasn't—

"Congratulations!"

Somebody poked me. Will Dietz whispered that I had the part. I hadn't heard Mr. Silverberry say ". . . played by Rachel Kahn."

I actually got it!

I grinned so hard my face almost split. I said, "I did? Really?" Then, out of nowhere, I flashed on telling Mom and Dad and my sister, Sara. I wondered if they'd pay attention.

At lunch my friends toasted me with Pepsi and Snapple and made up rave reviews and told me what to wear to the cast party. I spent the afternoon in a happy glow that even French class and Madame Miserable couldn't spoil.

111

When I got home, Mom was in the kitchen, working on dinner. I could have told her about getting the part then, but I wanted to tell everyone at once.

I looked for Sara. She's a senior in high school, and I'm a junior. We aren't close, maybe because we share a bedroom. *Share* isn't the right word. Our room is a demilitarized zone. We try not to escalate hostilities, and mostly we respect the rules of turf we've hammered out over the years.

Today she was actually home, studying in our bedroom. At least three nights a week she's late for dinner. Neither of us has to come home right after school, but we're supposed to tell Mom and Dad where we're going, and we're supposed to call if we're going to be late, and we're supposed to carry our beepers.

She usually strikes out on all three. When she's very late, which is often, my parents decide that she's been mugged. They always forget that the same thing happened two nights before and she turned up perfectly healthy ten minutes after they started calling all the hospitals in New York City.

On those nights when they're convinced Sara is bleeding into a sewer, it wouldn't matter if I had just won an Oscar. They would be completely uninterested.

I took my homework into the living room. When I heard Dad unlock our apartment door, I ran to meet him.

"What's wrong?" he said.

"Nothing. Can't I greet my father without anything being wrong?" I hugged him.

"This is nice." He hugged me back. He smelled

sweaty from the subway and cold because it was February.

I followed him while he hung up his coat and went into the kitchen to hug Mom. We have a family hug routine. We hug each other and pound each other on the back at the same time. This is normal at my house, when no crisis is going on.

Then my father went to the bathroom, and I set the table. Sara came into the kitchen, which should have clued me in that something was up. Usually when she's home, she stays in her room till Mom has yelled twice for her and my father's face has started to turn red.

I felt like it was all being choreographed for me.

My mother ladled soup, and I carried the bowls to the table.

"What's new with Jack?" Dad asked. Jack Phillips is the lunatic who runs the real estate agency where Mom works.

Mom took a deep breath, getting ready to answer, but I jumped in first. Jack Phillips stories are never short, and I couldn't wait.

"I got the part of Lavinia. It's the lead in *Androcles and the Lion,* the senior play."

They congratulated me. Sara said it was great. Dad smiled. Mom said she was going to be a nervous wreck watching me. Would she have preferred for me *not* to get the part?

And then my fifteen seconds of fame were over.

My mother said, "I made the soup too salty."

Dad said, "It's delicious, Laura."

Mom took another deep breath to start the Jack

Phillips story, but this time Sara jumped in. "I've been thinking about something." She smiled. "I want to tell you about it. It means a lot to me for you to be behind me."

They didn't see it coming. They just waited, no foreboding on their faces. But I knew trouble was on the way. I didn't know what it was going to be, but I thought, *Look out!* I don't know who I was warning. Me, probably.

"You know how you always tell me I need more structure?"

"We've said that once or twice," Mom said, smiling.

"Well, I've found the way to get it. I want to be baptized. I've decided to convert to Episcopalianism."

My father balled up his napkin and threw it on the table. His words slammed out. "Six million did not die so you could become a Gentile." He got up and left the kitchen.

We're Jewish. Not religious, but Dad's parents, who both died when I was very small, were Holocaust survivors. Dad sometimes talks about how hard it was to grow up with a mother and father who'd been in a concentration camp. When he got mad at them, he couldn't act mad—behave like an ordinary kid—because of what they'd been through.

After Dad left the room, Mom said, "He's afraid of what he'd do if he stayed."

"Doesn't he want to find out why I'm doing this? Don't you?"

I should have told my mother about the part as soon as I got home from school. I should have taken Dad aside separately too. That would have been the way to do it.

"What I want to find out is how you could do this to us." Mom started clearing the soup bowls. I stood up to help, and she said "thank you" politely, as if I were a stranger.

My father came back in. His lips were clamped together like he'd never talk again. Mom and I brought dishes to the table, cold chicken leftovers, baked potatoes, salad.

I had practiced for weeks, getting ready for the audition. I hadn't told Mom and Dad or Sara about it because I wanted to surprise them. And I didn't want them to think less of me if someone else got the part.

Sara said, "I thought you'd be glad I've found something that's bringing meaning to my life."

Dad turned red, and I was scared he'd have a heart attack. Mom started humming, and Sara finally found the sense to shut up.

Nobody talked for a few minutes, and then I told them about getting the part, about how I was sure Melissa Jordan would get it because she was a senior and she got the lead in everything. I talked about the rehearsal schedule and about how hard memorizing my lines was going to be, because Shaw plays have such long speeches. I didn't know why I was talking. They weren't listening, even though they pretended they were. So I also found the sense to shut up, and we finished eating in silence.

And then I thought of something funny. *Androcles and the Lion* is about religion. It's about a bunch of early

Christians who are waiting to be thrown to the lions for their beliefs.

If I thought Sara was anything like them—if I thought she honestly wanted to convert—I would have tried to help her. I would have stood up for her with Mom and Dad.

Not that she was faking. I was sure she believed she wanted to be an Episcopalian. But I was also sure that if you peeled back a dozen or so layers in my sister's crazy onion of a brain, you'd discover that what she really wanted was to stir up trouble and be the eye of my parents' cyclone.

It was like her lateness, only more so. When she arrives very late, after the hospital phone calls have begun, she always has a long string of explanations. Mom and Dad are always furious, and Sara always gets mad right back—because they won't sympathize with her tale of woe. It usually takes hours for the argument to simmer down and for them to forgive each other.

No one else ever seems to notice that Sara's explanations usually start with something avoidable—she lost her subway pass, she missed her train stop, she twisted her ankle. One story began with her getting soaked by a water fountain. A water fountain!

For the next few weeks home was hell. Mom and Dad made Sara talk to the rabbi at our synagogue (which we almost never attend). They made both of us go with them to a family therapist, where Mom and Dad and Sara did all the talking. Dr. Barone never asked me how I felt about the situation, although I thought he should have.

After all, I was a member of the family. Wasn't I?

Mom and Dad also got the name of an expert who talked kids out of being in cults. But the expert refused to talk to Sara. He said Episcopalianism wasn't a cult.

Meanwhile, rehearsals went well some days, not so good others. Sometimes it was lots of fun. Will, who played the lion (in a lion suit), had trouble getting his roar right, so the whole cast worked on it with him. I had a good roar. It reverberated in my chest and felt satisfying, extremely satisfying. When Will had perfected his roar, we worked with him on his purr. I liked purring, too. I liked the whole play. I pretty much memorized it, and sometimes when I was alone, I'd play all the parts.

Some things weren't so great, though. Mr. Silverberry kept nagging us to pick up the pace, which was hard, because Shaw plays are so wordy and the dialogue doesn't flow naturally.

Jason, who played Ferrovius, took forever to learn his part. Mr. Silverberry got mad at him at every rehearsal because he still had to carry his script around or get cued for almost every line. The cast was mad at him too. We might not have been fabulous actors, but at least we could memorize our lines.

Mr. Silverberry liked my interpretation of Lavinia, but he said I shouldn't emphasize every expression in my speeches. I should decide which were the most important and only stress them. So I tried, but I wasn't sure I was picking the right spots. I said my lines for my friend Alicia. We talked about what to accentuate, but I still wasn't certain.

I would have liked to ask Mom and Dad what they thought, but I didn't. I didn't exist for them these days. Oh, they were nice to me—*excruciatingly* nice—to make Sara feel how much out of favor she was by comparison. Sometimes they didn't speak to her. Sometimes they refused to let her do things she wanted to do. Sometimes they harangued her about how much she was hurting them. But when they yelled or even when they gave her the silent treatment, at least it was real.

So I didn't want to ask these fake nice people for help. They would only have said that I sounded good and they were sure I was remarkably talented. I might have screamed.

Then, about a month after her announcement, Sara told them she had changed her mind. She wasn't going to convert, but her decision had nothing to do with them. She simply wasn't certain that the Episcopal Church was the one true church. And if she had doubts, she thought it would be wrong to go through with it.

Mom and Dad didn't care why she changed her mind. The minute she changed it, the war was over. Everybody was happy again. The atmosphere lost its electric charge, and I stopped being scared of an explosion every time I walked into a room with Sara and my parents in it.

I still didn't talk about my role. I just practiced on my own and tried to make it as good as I could. Mr. Silverberry didn't criticize me again, so maybe it was better, or maybe he had given up.

And then the performance was a week away, and we all turned into nervous wrecks. I couldn't remember lines

I could have recited backward the week before. We mixed up the blocking. We missed our cues. Every word of our lines grew consonants, so that we couldn't pronounce anything right. We got the giggles and broke up whenever something went wrong, which was constantly.

Two days before dress rehearsal, Mr. Silverberry got so upset that instead of reading his notes at the end of the rehearsal, he said, "Forget it." He put on his coat and told us to go home.

That made us get serious. The next rehearsal was like a dream, smooth as satin. Everybody felt good, and everybody *was* good. Backstage we kept grinning at one another.

That rehearsal was the first time I *felt* my part. It was especially hard to in this play, which was ninety-nine percent intellectual. But that afternoon I did it. I caught Lavinia's zeal for God, for something bigger and more important than herself. It was amazing, thrilling—to find myself thinking a made-up person's thoughts, feeling her emotions, inhabiting her. I walked on air all the way home.

But then dress rehearsal was a disaster. Todd, who played the captain, my romantic interest (in real life I was definitely *not* interested), had caught a cold overnight. He kept sneezing, and he couldn't pronounce the letter *n*. I got the hiccups in the second act, and they gave me the giggles, which everybody else caught. Jason, who had finally learned his lines, couldn't remember half of them, and Will tripped over his tail on the steps leading to the offstage arena. He completely dropped out of character and started cursing. And near the end, Mike (who played Caesar) caught his cape on a nail, and it made a ripping sound that you could have heard a mile away.

Then it was over. Mr. Silverberry gave us our notes. "Boys and girls," he began sweetly, "dear children, here are my notes before they cart me off to a lunatic asylum." He started listing everything that had gone wrong, and his voice got less and less sweet and more and more loud. When he was done, he didn't say we could go. He sat quietly for a minute, and then he said, "I must really be insane. I can't give up. Look. Todd, Rachel, . . ."—he named five of us who had the biggest parts—"could you stay late? Maybe we can read through the play a few more times."

The five of us had to check home, but we all thought we could. So Mr. Silverberry told everybody else they could leave, and he gave us a half hour to call our parents and buy stuff from the candy and soda machines.

On my way down to the phone in the lobby it occurred to me not to call. Just to be late. I'd be the one who showed up hours after she was expected. I'd ignore my beeper and be the one my parents worried about. I turned around on the stairs and walked up an extra flight so I could be alone to think.

Mom and Dad would get scared about me sooner than they got scared about Sara because I was never late. I pictured it. Mom would be getting dinner ready. She'd wonder where I was. Dad would come home and I still wouldn't be there. Maybe Sara would be late too. I hoped she would be, because they wouldn't worry about her at all, not compared to me. They would panic. They'd call hospitals, and they'd babble about what a good child I was, how considerate, how utterly reliable. This was wonderful, like picturing my own funeral.

But then I had another thought, and before I even finished thinking it, I started crying. Sobbing my head off. Because I was sure they wouldn't remember I was in a play. I tried to catch my breath—I was sobbing and gasping. Sure, they would come to the performance when I reminded them. But I knew they'd forgotten I was going to be the female lead in the senior play. They had no idea that kids told me they thought I was a terrific actor, that I had worked harder on this part than I had ever worked on anything, that this was the most exciting thing that had happened to me since being born.

I stopped thinking and just cried. And felt terrible. And cried.

Finally my tears slowed down and stopped. Twenty minutes of our break had gone by. My nose was stuffed. My eyes had to be bloodshot. I stood up and headed for the bathroom so no one would see me till I washed my face.

If I didn't call, Mom and Dad would be frantic by the time I got home. I turned on the tap and splashed cold water into my eyes. They'd be furious, and the atmosphere would go back to explosive subzero, only it would be aimed at me, and Sara would be treated to a dose of bland politeness.

I didn't know how long it would last for one lateness. But I could probably stretch it out if I didn't apologize enough when I did get home. I could make things miserable for days.

There was a yellow water stain in the sink. I stared at it. Why did I want to be the center of a family crisis? Why did I want to be alternately yelled at and ignored? Why did I want whispered parental conferences about me? Why did I want them to watch me for clues to my behavior, as though I was a new arrival from the North Pole?

Why did I want the role of problem daughter? Even though Sara made trouble often, she didn't seem happy when Mom and Dad were mad at her. She wasn't enjoying herself, basking in the glare of their furious attention. I didn't enjoy it when I was ignored, but I didn't need to exchange one kind of misery for another, for a worse misery. And then I thought—and the thought astonished me—Sara wasn't a problem daughter. Not really. She was the victim of central casting for our family. Somebody had to create the crises, and she always stepped in and did it. I should be grateful, because I didn't want Sara's role. I already had a role, a better one—a real one—Lavinia in *Androcles and the Lion,* by George Bernard Shaw.

I combed my hair, feeling better, feeling good. Usually I'm exhausted after crying for a long time, but now I was energized. I put on fresh lipstick and left the bathroom. Since I did *not* want the family spotlight on me, I had to call home.

I preferred to be on the fringe—Pluto, not Mercury—of our family's solar system.

Of course it would be much better to have parents who paid attention to me, Rachel, just as I was. It would have been great to get Mom and Dad's help with my role, to feel that they were rooting for me. But it was good enough to be me, the one who had acting talent (some, anyway) and who had the lead in the school play. That was good enough all by itself.

I dialed. Mom answered. "Rachel? Where are you? I was getting worried."

"I'm still at school. I'll be home by eight thirty. We're having an extra rehearsal."

"Oh. What are you rehearsing?"

I started laughing. "It's the school play, and I have the lead."

"Oh. That's right. I forgot."

"I have to go. I'm late. Bye."

I headed back to the auditorium. Curtain up!

Gail Carson Levine

The way to get my parents' attention when my sister and I were kids was to have a problem or to be a problem. My sister and I often created problems, because if we didn't, we were sidelined and the spotlight moved elsewhere, usually to trouble with my mother's difficult family.

So much young adult literature lately seems to be about terribly distressing families. We read tales of abuse, of addiction, of madness. I know there are such families, but I wanted to show in "Pluto" that even loving families have quirks, and maybe a bit more than quirks. Growing up is hard, and teenagers in loving families still have to make tough choices about the people they want to become.

In high school I did have the lead in *Androcles and the Lion,* but my sister never threatened to become an Episcopalian. I was interested in acting and painting, not in writing. I discovered that I'm a writer when I took a class in writing and illustrating for children, and found that I loved the writing and loathed the illustrating. I've been writing for twelve years now, full-time for about two years. I also volunteer at the local middle school, teaching creative writing to kids who've been bitten by the writing bug. "Pluto" is the first short story I've written since high school! I grew up in New York City and now live about fifty miles to the north, in a two-hundred-year-old farmhouse with my husband, David, and our Airedale, Jake.

Gail Carson Levine is the author of seven books for children and young adults. Her first book, *Ella Enchanted,* was a Newbery Honor Book in 1998, and has won Readers Choice Awards in Vermont, Maine, and Arizona. More recently, she has published four fairy tale books in The Princess Tales series: *The Fairy's Mistake, The Princess Test, Princess Sonora and the Long Sleep,* and *Cinderellis and the Glass Hill.* In the fall of 1999 she released her historical novel, *Dave at Night,* which is loosely based on her father's childhood in an orphanage in New York City. And in the spring of 2000 *The Wish,* her contemporary fairy tale about popularity, appeared in bookstores.

She was more nervous about performing now than she had ever been in her life. She had checked her shoes, she had checked the spot for Vaseline, and both were fine. But something else could still happen, something she wasn't expecting, like both times before.

She was trembling as they danced, but she was also determined. It wasn't as perfect as it had been at the beginning last night, but it went well enough. She began to hope that this time nothing would happen—maybe Helen had run out of tricks. And afterward they would confront her, and that would be the end of it.

Unbalanced

by William Sleator

"Oh, that was close!" she gasped, just offstage, bent over with her hands on her knees, gulping air. "If you weren't so quick, it would have been a fracture for sure."

He rested his hand lightly, comfortingly on her shoulder. "I'm there for you," he said, breathing as hard as she was. "I just want to know who made that place slippery."

Linda felt the panic, which had just been subsiding, start to rise again. "You think somebody put Vaseline there on purpose?"

"How else did it get there?" Jimmy said.

They ran out to take their bows.

It was a bad, tricky step. She had to run toward the specific place upstage left, marked with a piece of tape, which would be right under the follow spotlight, and then suddenly stop, on pointe, in arabesque, one leg out behind her. It was hard, but she had finally got it in rehearsal. Tonight, in performance, she had reached the place and gone up on pointe. But this time there was no friction to stop her—her foot was sliding horribly out from under her, her arms flailing. She was going over backward, her spine heading for the stage.

129

Jimmy rushed out of the choreography, lifted her before she fell, and carried her offstage for their exit.

Back in the wing, their bows over, she asked, "But why would somebody do that to me?" Her breath was coming easier now, but the sweat on her body chilled her. "What did I ever do to anybody?" Her voice sounded like a little girl's.

Which she nearly was. To be a soloist at seventeen was unusual. All those long years at ballet school, and then acceptance by the company at fifteen, and two years later—last week, in fact—promotion to soloist. Maybe she was naive, but she thought promotion meant people were on her side.

"You haven't learned yet?" Jimmy said. "You don't know what they're like here?" He stood up now, tall and beautiful. He was twenty-five and a principal dancer, the highest level. "There are other people who wanted to get promoted to soloist, who've been in the company longer than you. Older than you. They could do anything. You've got to know that. You've got to . . . watch out for it."

She tightened. It had been magical being promoted so soon, a dream. Now suddenly what it meant was fear.

"Linda, what happened?" It was Carla, her best friend in the company.

"Somebody put Vaseline on the stage," Jimmy said, looking hard at Carla, his voice dead calm. "And I'm going to find out who, and I'm going to kill her. See you in class tomorrow." He strode away.

They were in different dressing rooms now—Carla had not been promoted from the corps. But they lived close enough to each other to walk partway home together. Carla was twenty-two, and she had taken Linda under her wing. "Jimmy really thinks somebody's out to get you?" Carla asked her, walking through the leaves on the sidewalk.

"He says it's because I got promoted and other people who've been in the company longer didn't." She shook her head. "But it's not my fault. I can't help it if Maggie promoted me. I didn't walk over anybody to make it happen."

"They don't care," Carla said, her face hard. Linda knew how unhappy Carla had been when she found out she hadn't been promoted, but it didn't seem to change her feelings for Linda. She squeezed Linda's shoulder. "Jimmy's watching out for you, and I am too," she said warmly. "We'll find out who it is and stop her. I don't want you worrying about it. You've got to concentrate on dancing now, more than ever."

Linda didn't sleep well. It would be very easy for someone to put Vaseline on the stage. All the girls had Vaseline. They wore it on their lips, inside and out, during performance, so that when their mouth got dry, their lips wouldn't stick to their teeth, giving their stage smile a snaggle-toothed look. Before the show the stage was always swarming with dancers, warming up and practicing steps. Whoever had done it would most likely not have been noticed.

In class the next morning, at the barre, she looked around at the thirty-six dancers in the company, twenty-four of them female. Everyone was rumpled, sloppy in baggy, unraveling leg warmers and old, falling-apart slippers. Which one was it?

She could rule out the four principal girls—they were above her and had no reason to feel competitive or envious. The same was true of the four other soloists, who routinely had better parts than she did. She could rule out Carla, her best friend. That left the fourteen other girls in the corps. Which ones had been hoping to get promoted? Which one was desperate and cruel enough to try to injure her so she could take her place?

Dora and Eloise were reputed to be almost thirty. They were too old to have any hope of getting out of the corps now. A lot of the others were so young and fresh that they were still thrilled to be in the company at all— they had time and didn't need to do anything drastic to get ahead. So that left . . .

Her eyes fixed on Helen, then quickly slipped away before Helen noticed, looking straight ahead now as she sank down into a *grande plié*. Helen was twenty-three. Helen was a good dancer. Helen didn't have a lot of friends. She was cool and inward. She lived with her boyfriend, a law student, and kept away from company parties. Was it her?

Before the performance that night, onstage behind the closed curtain, Linda and Jimmy went through some of their lifts and catches. Jimmy was a wonderful partner, attuned to her body, right on the music, always gentle, never rough like some of the less experienced boys. It was so reassuring to have a partner like Jimmy, since she was so small and your partner was in complete control when you were dancing.

The applause for the conductor rose up, the signal to get off the stage just before curtain. In the wing she whispered to him, "Do you think it could be Helen?"

He looked down at her—he was almost six feet, and she was five two—and furrowed his brow. "She *is* getting old to be in the corps, if she wants to have a real career," he murmured. "And she's good. If you weren't around, they probably would have promoted her. I'll ask Al if he noticed her doing anything unusual before the performance last night." He stepped away, muscles moving under his tight unitard.

Al was the dancer-friendly stagehand, the one who seemed to regard all of them as his children. Linda waited nervously, pacing. She always had a certain amount of stage fright, but that was normal; it gave you the adrenaline to do your best. But now she had an extra and very real worry: What was going to happen tonight when she ran for that spot?

Was there time to check it out? Why hadn't she thought of this before? They weren't supposed to be onstage now; in an instant the conductor would raise his baton and the curtain would go up. But she had a few seconds. She dashed onto the stage and over to the tape. She bent over and felt the stage with her hand. It was tacky, from all the rosin on the dancers' shoes. No Vaseline tonight, within a foot of the spot. And too late for anybody to put it there. She heard the deep *swoosh* of the curtain opening and rushed back into the wings just in time.

Jimmy was waiting for her as the music began. "It's clean," she said. "What did Al say?"

Jimmy looked grim. "He saw Helen backstage with a jar of Vaseline last night, but he sees that all the time. He didn't notice her doing anything unusual onstage before the show. No help."

They stepped aside as a line of corps girls ran out on stage, led by Helen.

"Did you tell him what happened so he can watch out for it?" Linda whispered.

"No. I don't want to say anything until I'm sure. But I did ask him to keep his eye out for anybody bringing Vaseline onstage. He knew enough not to ask why." He touched her elbow comfortingly. "So you checked the spot? That was smart of you. I did too, before you came up. Don't worry, Lindy. I hate to see you look worried. Everything's going to be okay. We'll stop this. I'm here for you." He paused. "Maggie say anything to you about last night?"

Maggie was Margaret Stephens, the artistic director, the boss. All the dancers called her Maggie behind her back. "No. She didn't. But she must have noticed and thought it was my fault. And she just promoted me! I've got to make up for it tonight."

The beginning of their dance went better tonight than last night—the nerves might be good for both of them. The hardest part—except for Linda's run to arabesque—was the lift in the slow section. Jimmy held her above him upside down, and then she had to slowly slide down his body to the floor. He lifted one arm and used the other hand to guide and support her from behind, unseen by the audience. She had to keep both hands up in the air, against the natural instinct to hold them down and in front of her to protect her in case she slipped—that was the beauty of the step, her hands in the air as she slithered down him headfirst toward the floor. Tonight it went so smoothly, no jerks, no fumbling, his invisible hand keeping her safe and steady. They had never done it that well before, even in rehearsal. No other partner she had ever danced with could have guided and protected her so well.

Her torso made gentle contact with the floor, her hands still lifted. Then he pulled her up and she ran upstage right to start her hops on pointe.

Thirty-two hops on one toe, moving diagonally across the stage, the other leg held in the air in front of her. The audience always went nuts over this step, but she had practiced it so many times that it didn't unnerve her anymore.

And then the ribbons fell off—the ribbons that attached the shoe she was hopping on to her foot.

Toe shoes came without ribbons. Dancers spent a lot of time sewing ribbons to the shoes. The shoe had to be part of the foot in order to support you in the highly unnatural and difficult position of being on pointe. The ribbons were what made the shoe part of the foot, sewn to the shoe and then carefully and tightly tied around the ankle.

And now the ribbons had come off. The shoe she was hopping in was not part of her foot, it was a floppy appendage, giving her no support. She tried to keep on hopping, but she could feel that in a matter of seconds her wobbling ankle would give way, it could fracture, she would fall—unless she just stopped in the middle of the step.

But that was impossible. She couldn't do that, what would Maggie say—two mistakes onstage on two consecutive nights, just after being promoted. She couldn't stop the hops.

But if she kept them up, she would be injured. Her heart was thudding, she was trembling, her ankle was screaming in pain, the shoe felt like it was about to fall off.

And then Jimmy was beside her, lifting her gently, setting her down on both flat feet, nudging her into an easy *balancee* waltz step. The audience wouldn't know anything was wrong. Maggie would, but at least she hadn't been injured. And—thank God!—the run into arabesque, the one that was safe to do tonight, was on the foot with the good shoe. She did it perfectly.

Jimmy had saved her again.

Backstage after the bows she pulled off the shoe. "I *know* I sewed these on as good as ever!" she said. And the neat, tiny stitches were all there. She and Jimmy and Carla examined the ribbon just above the stitches, where it had broken.

"Smooth," Carla murmured. "Smooth almost all the way across, and then ragged. She cut your ribbons, Lindy. Not enough so you would notice, but enough so they'd break when there was a lot of pressure on them."

Now it was a struggle for Linda to hold back her tears. "What am I going to do? Something different every night! How do I know what to look for next, what to be afraid of?"

For a long moment Jimmy's and Carla's eyes met. It was as though they were making a silent pact to protect her. "It won't happen again," Jimmy said. "We'll take care of that."

They were older, they had been dancing longer, and they were going to protect her. At least she had that going for her.

Maggie spoke to her after class the next morning, when the other dancers were leaving the studio. "Twice in two nights you almost fell onstage, Linda," Maggie said, shaking her head. "You're lucky Jimmy was fast enough to save you both times—if it weren't for him, you would have made a fool of yourself, and me. If anything else happens, you're never doing that part again. I hope it wasn't a mistake to promote you."

"But . . . but it wasn't my fault," Linda couldn't keep from saying, though it sounded so babyish.

"Whose fault could it have been then, may I ask?" Maggie said coldly. She was fat—though she was always telling the dancers *they* were too fat—and she wore a smocklike dress that barely reached her knees, to show off what she thought were her good legs.

"I don't know who," Linda said. "But somebody put Vaseline on the stage the first night, and last night my ribbons were cut."

Maggie lifted her chin angrily. "Things like that don't happen in my company," she said. "Don't blame your own mistakes on childish imaginary enemies. You do a perfect performance tonight, or else. Understood?" She turned and walked away.

"We're going to confront Helen tonight, after the show," Carla told her backstage before the performance.

She had just told Jimmy and Carla what Maggie had said—and how Maggie had noticed that Jimmy had saved her both times.

"You probably shouldn't have said anything to her about the Vaseline and the ribbons before you had proof of who did it," Jimmy said kindly. "Maggie doesn't like to think about things like that."

"But tonight we'll get Helen to admit," Carla re-assured her again. "And then . . ." She ran her finger across her throat.

She was more nervous about performing now than she had ever been in her life. She had checked her shoes, she had checked the spot for Vaseline, and both were fine. But something else could still happen, something she wasn't expecting, like both times before.

She was trembling as they danced, but she was also determined. It wasn't as perfect as it had been at the beginning last night, but it went well enough. She began to hope that this time nothing would happen—maybe Helen had run out of tricks. And afterward they would confront her, and that would be the end of it.

Jimmy lifted her. He positioned her tiny body upside down in front of his tall torso. He held his left hand in the air and with his right began easing her slowly down his body. She kept her hands lifted.

And then he let go of her.

Her head hit the floor, hard. She felt something snap at the top of her neck. And then she didn't feel anything else at all.

The music stopped. Murmurs and cries of alarm

reached her from the audience. Jimmy knew enough not to move her. The curtain came down. And she was thinking, *Nobody will ever believe he did this. He saved me two times before.*

Dancers hovered around her until the stretcher came. Helen was especially kind and concerned, bringing a wet towel for her face, comforting her.

As they bore her away in the stretcher, her head lying limply to one side, she saw Jimmy and Carla walk away together.

Holding hands.

William Sleator

Information about my early life—important things such as how cleverly I tormented my little brothers—can be found in my book *Oddballs*. So here I want to mention the time I spent working as a rehearsal pianist for a ballet company.

I had this job for nine years, at the same time I was starting out as a writer. Even though I was publishing books, I was still not making enough money from writing to support myself—that's how the profession is—so I worked for the ballet company, and wrote books when I was not playing the piano in the rehearsal studio. I watched performances from backstage and took notes—writing down what the dancers said to one another *while* they were dancing—and also took many, many notes on the tours we dragged across America and Europe.

The events in this story did not actually happen, as far as I know. But they could have. Ballet appears glamorous, but it is a grueling and cutthroat profession. "Unbalanced" is only the beginning of the stories I could tell, which I hope to write someday. And when I do—they will be no less gruesome.

William Sleator's most recent novels are *Rewind* and *Boltzmon!* Though he has won numerous awards for many other books, such as *Singularity* (his personal favorite), he is most proud of winning the California Young Reader Medal, voted for by the high school students of California, for *Interstellar Pig*.

Brandon fell to the sand, threw his head back, and howled at the sky until he was hoarse. He caught his breath, shuddering, but couldn't stand. His right foot was caught. As he yanked it free the sand made a sucking noise, like someone slurping a soda with a straw, and he lost his shoe. He groped for it, but it had disappeared without a trace. The wet sand tugged at his hand like something alive. "What the hell—" He inched forward and his other foot sank. "Shit," he whispered. His foot came out, but no shoe.

Sables mouvants, *he thought.* I get it. . . .

Sables Mouvants

by Liza Ketchum

For Sally

Brandon McGinnis let the crowd of Parisian commuters carry him up the Metro escalator and out into the street, slick with rain. He must look like an idiot, with this grin plastered across his face—but why should he care? He'd fallen for Paris in the springtime, just like that sappy song Dad used to sing. If he stayed long enough, maybe he could forget this whole last year.

Fat chance, Brandon thought. He nodded at the bartender in the corner café, where he drank a *café crème* every morning, then sidled past the sidewalk oven, his mouth watering over the chickens roasting on a spit inside. He dodged a woman carrying her fresh baguette under one arm, and stopped at the corner market to inspect the colorful banks of fruit and vegetables. As if I lived here, Brandon thought. But who was he kidding? Anyone could tell he was a tourist, with his terrible French, his Irish complexion, and his Boston Red Sox jacket.

He crossed the wet courtyard and climbed the steep flights of stairs to their friend's apartment. The place was quiet. "Anybody home?" Brandon called.

143

"Down here!" His mother's voice echoed along the hall. Brandon tossed his windbreaker on the couch and slicked his hair back. Mom's friend Cheryl was working late tonight. Maybe we'll go out to eat, Brandon thought. His stomach growled happily at the thought.

He stopped dead in the door of the guest room. Something was up. His grandfather sat on the bed, his suitcase open beside him. "You leaving, Pop?"

"Not exactly." His grandfather held out a green guidebook to Normandy.

Brandon glanced at his mother, who shrugged. "Pop has always wanted to visit the D-day beaches," she said.

"Beaches in *April?*" Brandon laughed. "Pop, I know you're dying for topless French girls, but it's pretty chilly."

Pop rolled his eyes at his daughter. "What did I tell you? No one learns history anymore. He's never heard of D day."

"Wait a minute," Brandon said, "I know that one. World War Two."

"Good for you." Pop cleaned his glasses on his shirt-tail. "My best friend, Sam Friedman, was killed in the landing. I thought I'd go up for a night or two—maybe visit his grave."

Brandon's gut tightened. A cemetery? Forget it. He didn't need that now. "You and Mom should go, Pop. Cheryl won't mind if I stay here alone."

"Your mother and Cheryl have plans," Pop said. "Besides, I need a navigator." He tossed him the guide-book. "Pick a place you'd like to see while we're there."

Before he could protest, Brandon caught the warning look in his mother's eye. He was trapped. "When do we leave?" he asked, trying to swallow his anger.

"First thing in the morning," Pop said.

Brandon was dozing in his sleeping bag when his mother came in and perched on the end of the couch.

"That was a nasty trick, Mom," Brandon said. "You could have asked me first."

"I'm sorry." She squeezed cream into her hand and rubbed her palms together. "Pop paid for our vacation, and he never mentioned Normandy. He shouldn't go alone." She patted his knee. "You and Pop could use some private time together."

Brandon groaned. "Wake up, Mom. Pop doesn't help. He acts like Dad died on purpose. Besides, I thought we came here to forget all that stuff."

"We did." His mother wouldn't meet his eyes. "Most people would give anything to visit Normandy. You're only seventeen; you can always come back to Paris. Pop's getting old. It might be his last trip."

Brandon didn't want to think about anyone else dying. He reached for his Discman and slipped in a Phish CD. "Okay. But there's no way I'll visit the cemetery. Pop's on his own with that one."

The next morning Brandon sat in their rented car, a tiny blue box called a Twingo, with the map open on his knees. How did he get into this? His grandfather was white-knuckling the steering wheel as French semis

Sables Mouvants   **145**

roared past, spewing curtains of water over the windshield. "You see all right, Pop?" Brandon asked. The clatter of the wipers drowned Pop's answer.

The car sucked in exhaust like a vacuum cleaner. Brandon cracked the window and glanced at his watch. Mom and Cheryl would be sitting in the corner café now, sipping their *café crèmes*. French girls in tight black skirts and platform shoes would hustle past, but Mom wouldn't even notice. Brandon sighed.

Outside the city limits his grandfather relaxed and talked about the importance of D day, how it was the biggest invasion of troops ever, the beginning of the end for the Germans. Brandon only half listened until Pop said, "I should have been here."

Brandon stared at him. "Where were you?" He felt stupid. He'd never asked Pop what he did in the war.

Pop pointed to his thick glasses. "My eyes were always bad. I had a desk job, decoding enemy messages."

"That sounds pretty important." Brandon grinned at his grandfather. "Sorry to be rude, but you don't seem like the spy type."

Pop smiled. "True. You forget I'm good at puzzles and word games."

"Was it exciting?"

"Once in a while—when we broke a code. Most of the time we were bored—or scared. If we gave our troops false information, we sent them to die."

"Wasn't it better to sit at a desk, instead of getting shot at?"

"We didn't think so." Pop's voice was bitter. "We felt

like cowards. Crazy—we half envied the guys who died. *They* were heroes. And the ones who came home had exciting stories to tell. Our war was boring compared to theirs."

"Hey. If you'd been killed over here, you wouldn't have had Mom, and she wouldn't have had *me*," Brandon teased. He poked Pop gently, eager to change the subject. "Who would have tested the new treats in your bakery, if I hadn't been born?" Pop smiled and Brandon relaxed. War could be a dicey topic in his family.

As they neared the coast, the rain slowed to a drizzle and clouds lifted over newly plowed fields. Pop pulled up at the top of a hill and they looked down on the sleepy town of Arromanches-les-Bains, tucked next to the sea. "Where did the troops come in?" Brandon asked.

"All along the coast. They brought a whole damned port over in pieces from England and put it together almost overnight. Took the Germans by surprise." Pop whistled through his teeth, pointing at a sheer headland rising from the waves a few miles up the coast. "That must be Pointe du Hoc, where Sam died."

"They scaled those *cliffs*?" Brandon asked. "Why?"

"The Germans were dug in there, with heavy artillery," Pop said. "We'll check it out after the museum."

Brandon had to admit the museum wasn't half bad. There were films showing the construction of the harbor, and a slide show that made him feel part of the invasion, with planes buzzing overhead and thousands of guys pouring onto the beaches. The displays of uniforms, letters, and old photos stopped him in his tracks. Those guys were my age, he thought, staring at one cocky guy in an RAF uniform. He couldn't imagine Pop that young.

Brandon slipped outside and stood on the break-water, zipping his jacket against the wind. His father's old Red Sox jacket was threadbare, but Brandon wasn't ready to throw it out. Its musty smell brought back memories of playing catch with Dad on their Somerville street. He remembered Dad's quick grin, his hair already gray because he was older than most fathers. But then his green eyes would zero in on the plate; he'd blister a pitch into Brandon's waiting glove—and suddenly his father was as young and strong as Pedro Martinez.

Brandon quit Little League in third grade to become a swimmer. Dad was disappointed, but he still came to every meet. Brandon loved racing against the clock, loved the sleek feel of water against his skin, the shriek of the whistle echoing off the tiles. Too bad the sea here was so cold and gray—otherwise, he'd be tempted.

After a lunch of steamed mussels and french fries, Brandon jogged along Omaha Beach, a wide, sandy expanse, which cleared his head. But his heart sank when Pop said, "Check the map—I think the cemetery is nearby."

Sure enough, there it was: CIMETIÈRE MILITAIRE USA—you didn't need to know French to figure that one out.

Crowds of tourists scurried across the parking lot under umbrellas; it was raining again. Brandon hunkered down in his seat. "Brandon." Pop's gnarled hand was heavy on his knee. "Come see this with me."

Brandon couldn't meet Pop's eyes. "Sorry. It's too soon."

"I understand. But this—" Pop cleared his throat. "It's a moment in history that changed the world."

Brandon fidgeted in his seat, suddenly annoyed. "Give me a break, Pop. Dad's been dead less than a year."

Pop's blue eyes were cold when he was angry. He fumbled for the door handle. "You can't run away all your life, just because your father did."

Not that again. Brandon sank back in the tiny seat, as drained as if he'd just finished a hundred-meter freestyle event. "Get over it, Pop. So Dad went to Canada. *His* war sucked. Yours didn't." His voice shook. "Dad's dead, Pop. You can't fight him anymore. It's over. History."

"You wish." Pop slammed the door and lurched across the wet pavement. He'd forgotten his cane, but Brandon was too pissed to care.

What the hell was Pop's problem? Brandon's knee jumped and twitched. He cracked a window and pulled on his headset, but he couldn't focus on the music. Thoughts whined in his skull like Phish's electric guitar. Pop had always disapproved of Dad—his protests against the war, long before Brandon was born; his politics; his social worker jobs that "forced my daughter to work too hard"—at least that's how Pop put it. Never mind that Mom *liked* teaching. But his grandfather seemed even madder at Dad since he died, as if he'd crashed the car on purpose.

Of course, falling asleep at the wheel was a stupid thing to do, Brandon thought. He sighed. He'd been happy in Paris, for the first time in months. Why did Pop have to ruin it now?

Sables Mouvants **149**

Brandon dozed off, then startled awake to find his grandfather fumbling with the door. Pop fell into his seat, his scalp showing pink under his thin, matted hair.

Brandon yanked off the headset. "Pop—what's wrong?"

His grandfather started the car with a trembling hand. He stalled twice as they lurched across the parking lot. Brandon dug his nails into his palms. If only he were allowed to drive here! "Hey, Pop," he said, "how about stopping for coffee? There must be a place in the next town."

Pop's silence stung him like a slap across the face.

They drove to Pointe du Hoc without speaking. Pop grabbed his cane and made a beeline for the cliffs, stumping around the deep craters left by exploded shells, his head tucked against the wind. Brandon followed at a careful distance, avoiding the ruined bunkers, their concrete stairs disappearing into cold darkness. His grandfather's face was a chalky white, like the foam spewing over the rocks below the headland.

Brandon read a plaque describing how the Texas Rangers had scaled the cliffs with ropes and ladders; only half of them made it. He peered over the railing at the angry sea below. No way he could be that brave: to climb slick, wet rocks while German artillery pounded him from above—forget it.

Pop gazed out at the horizon. Brandon started toward him, then backed off. He didn't know how to fix what was wrong between them. Instead he walked back to the car as the wind keened through the exposed bunkers.

They drove west across the peninsula and spent the night in a farmhouse that rented rooms. In the morning Brandon pulled back the curtains and whistled under his breath. The sky had cleared and the bay sparkled in the morning light. In the distance, shimmering like a mirage, sat Mont-St-Michel, the abbey he'd read about in the guidebook. The church rose on its craggy island like a fantasy castle, topped by a spire reaching for the sky.

They had coffee and croissants at a small café on the beach promenade. It was warm enough to eat outside. Pop was quiet and Brandon kept his eyes on the bay. The tide was sliding away from the shore like a sheet pulled off a bed. Brandon pointed to the abbey. "Could we go out there this morning?" Brandon asked.

Pop only grunted. Brandon spooned up the last bit of foam from his cup and took a deep breath. "So, Pop—how come you're still so pissed at Dad?"

Pop's face reddened. "I'm sorry. It burned me up yesterday to think how Sam Friedman gave his life for his country—while your father burned his draft card and ran away."

"You think Dad was a coward." Brandon tried to keep his cool. "Know what, Pop? I think he was brave—*and* smart. Vietnam was a lousy war, and he knew it. Your friend stood up for what he believed in. So did Dad."

"I'm afraid not." Pop pushed his cup away. "Your father wasn't the saint you've built him up to be."

Brandon forced a smile. "Who is?"

Pop's mouth was set in a grim line. "Your father ran away from more than the war. In 1977, when President Carter declared amnesty for draft dodgers, your dad came home." Pop balled up his napkin, then met Brandon's eyes. "He left a child behind in Canada."

Brandon slammed his fist on the table, making the cups jump. "What the hell are you talking about?" He felt the café's sudden silence but didn't care. He glared at his grandfather. "Dad would never hide something like that from me."

Pop's face was as white as the plastic table shaking under his hands. "He hid it from everyone. Even your mother." Pop cleared his throat. "After your father died, there was a reading of the will, in the lawyer's office. And you didn't want to go. Remember?"

Of course he remembered. It was a school day, a week after the accident. He couldn't deal, and Dad didn't have much to give away. So he let Pop take Mom over there. She came back shaken up, but what else was new? After all, they were both wrecks most of the time—and she'd told him what he expected: Dad had left her nothing but debts. "So what happened?" Brandon asked now.

Pop took a long, slow breath. "Your father had written a letter—for his son, in Canada. In case—"

The words hit Brandon's chest like a heavy sandbag. He couldn't breathe. He jumped up, knocking over his chair, and bolted, ignoring Pop's hoarse cries. His sneakers slapped the concrete path beside the beach as he dodged women with strollers, old men with canes who stared at him with open mouths. He ran a long way to the end of the promenade, where he leaned over the railing, gasping for breath. Who was Dad, anyway? The guy who yelled the loudest at swim meets, who tossed him the car keys the night he got his license, no questions asked? Or some creep on a Wanted poster for deadbeat dads? Jesus. Dad hated fathers who gave up on their kids. Or so he'd said.

Brandon paced up and down. This was too crazy. He had a brother somewhere? A horrible thought twisted his gut. Was Dad married, or not? Pop hadn't even said. Brandon slid under the railing, fell to his knees, and vomited into the sand.

When he finally stood up, the tide was out, leaving the bay as scoured and empty as his stomach. Mont-St-Michel shimmered in the distance, remote and beckoning. He stood up and ran toward the abbey, jogging past groups of men and women raking the beach for shellfish. He glanced at a sign stuck into the sand, which read *SABLES MOUVANTS*. What did that mean? Something moving? Tides, maybe. He kept going. Pop could rot in that stinking café.

Half a mile from shore he doubled over with a stitch in his side. As he straightened up, two jet-black horses came trotting toward him, each one pulling a sulky. Brandon stared as they clipped past, their necks curved high and proud, tails flying in the wind, the wheels of their carts cleaving the sand with four deep tracks. He waved to the drivers, but they sat as still as crash-test dummies in a new car. The horses followed the curve of the shore toward the next town. They must be trotters, he thought, racers. If only he could run that fast, away from the thoughts pulsing like lasers through his skull.

He kept jogging, headed for the silver spire of the abbey. This was crazy; he couldn't run that far. But he couldn't deal with Pop either. The whole bay had emptied, as if someone had pulled out the plug. How long before the tide turned?

He passed a tractor towing a boat on wheels, the boat filled to the brim with oysters. The driver shouted at him, gesturing toward the outer bay. Brandon nodded, although he couldn't hear what the guy was saying.

The sand grew heavy and wet. He slowed to a walk and glanced behind him. He was a long way from shore, and now he could see something gold glinting on top of the abbey spire. He must be closer. He pushed ahead until his ears rang. As if it were yesterday, the ringing became the incessant shriek of the phone call that shattered his life. He saw his bedroom door swing open, his mother standing there, her thin body lit from behind, her hand clapped over her mouth—

Brandon fell to the sand, threw his head back, and howled at the sky until he was hoarse. He caught his breath, shuddering, but couldn't stand. His right foot was caught. As he yanked it free the sand made a sucking noise, like someone slurping a soda with a straw, and he lost his shoe. He groped for it, but it had disappeared without a trace. The wet sand tugged at his hand like something alive. "What the hell—" He inched forward and his other foot sank. "Shit," he whispered. His foot came out, but no shoe.

Sables mouvants, he thought. *I get it. Quicksand.*

He peeled off his socks and tried to run toward the shore, but the sand was saturated with seawater. He stumbled and fell to his hands and knees, scrambled to stable ground again and stood, gasping for breath. His jeans were heavy, as if he'd fallen into wet concrete.

Brandon searched frantically for his tracks. There they were—but he didn't trust his footing. He avoided the first soft spot but sank in another one. When he pulled himself out, he was shaking. "Oh, my God. What's happening?" He glanced behind him, toward the abbey. The tide was coming in.

For a second he thought he might crap in his pants. Was that why the tractor guy had yelled at him? Where was the tractor, anyway? He shielded his eyes. The bay was empty. Even the people digging close to shore had disappeared. "I'm dead meat," Brandon whispered.

Walking as fast as he dared, he heard a soft rippling sound behind him, like a crowd of people whispering. He broke into a slow jog, ignoring the shinsplints burning the fronts of his legs. He dodged the wet spots, but maybe the dry sand was just as bad—how could you tell? He peered over his shoulder. Was he paranoid, or was the tide gaining on him? Maybe he could ride it in. But the currents must be wicked here. Even his strongest flutter kick wouldn't help with this one.

The sand gave way without warning. This time he was in up to his knees. He swore, struggling, but his legs were caught. He flailed with his arms and suddenly, as if he were standing over him, he heard his swim coach, his steady voice saying: *Breathe. The secret is all in the breathing.* Brandon took two long, deep breaths, then another, determined to stay upright. He squinted and saw movement along the shore. The horses!

He screamed and pulled off his jacket, waving it overhead. The sound of rushing water grew closer. Damn—what was "help" in French? *"Au secours!"* he screamed at the top of his lungs. The horses kept on trotting, their tails lifted, their drivers tiny ants in the distance. Desperate, he put his fingers between his teeth and whistled, a shrill, frantic note, the trick Dad had taught him when he was little. He kept it up, whistling and screaming, until his tongue was dry. Finally—so gradually it seemed like he'd hit the slow-motion button on a VCR—one horse turned its head. He waved his jacket, a grimy blue flag, then dropped it and whistled again. He was deeper in the sand now, up to his thighs—and the tide was catching up to him.

The first horse slowed, then the second. Even from here he could feel their drivers hesitate. *"Au secours!"* he cried. At last they wheeled toward him in tandem.

He glanced over his shoulder. The water rippled across the sand, gobbling it up. No way the horses would come in time. He had to save himself. He unzipped his jeans and slithered out of them like a snake leaving its skin, then tossed his jacket in front of him and half swam, half crawled onto the wet cloth. He found steady ground at last and staggered to his feet, shivering in his boxers.

The horses were trotting fast, the sulkies bucking and swaying—and then suddenly, the drivers drew up. The horses pranced in place as the men beckoned and shouted. Brandon couldn't hear the words, but he understood: They couldn't come any closer.

The tide rushed at him, as if someone had opened the sluice on a dam. He took a deep breath, waited until the icy water swirled over his knees, then gritted his teeth and swam. Feet kicking hard, arms churning, eyes smarting with salt, he yearned for the buzzer to tell him he'd reached the end of the pool and won the heat—

Then his knees hit solid ground, and one horse was within reach. He scrambled toward the sulky. The horse shied and sidestepped, its eyes wild with terror, its black withers foamy with sweat. The driver let loose a torrent of French, gesturing at the back of the sulky. Brandon jumped up and hung on. He looped his fingers through the guy's belt, his toes gripped the axle, and they whirled to follow the second horse.

"Merci, merci," Brandon shouted. The horses raced the tide all the way in, the sulky's wheels clattering and wobbling until Brandon thought the fragile cart would splinter. Nothing, he decided, would ever be as beautiful as the sight of those black horses galloping toward him across the sand.

As they neared the shore a rescue jeep hurtled to meet them, blue lights popping and swirling. The driver reined in his horse, helped Brandon down, and then jumped out, grabbing the bridle. A crowd huddled on the promenade. Brandon glanced down at his wet boxers. What the hell—this was France, home of the topless bikini. He laughed, his teeth chattering.

Sables Mouvants   **157**

At the edge of the crowd, hands crossed over his chest, was Pop. Without a word, Brandon gripped him hard, burrowing his head into his grandfather's shoulder like a baby.

A few hours later, after they'd thanked the horsemen and the tractor driver—who'd called the police—and convinced the medic that Brandon only needed dry clothes and a shower, they sat in the same café where their day had started, in a booth at the back. The bartender brought them tea laced with rum before Pop even had a chance to order. Brandon shivered in Pop's old khakis and sweatshirt. Dad's jacket was lost to the tide.

Brandon cupped both hands around the mug to warm them. "I'm sorry I ran off," he said. "I couldn't deal with what you told me. It still seems like a bad dream."

"I know," Pop said. "There was no good way to break the news."

"That's okay." Brandon sipped his tea. "I just don't get it. Why did Dad keep it a secret?"

"Shame, I guess," Pop said. "If you had only let me finish this morning—the letter gave us some clues. Sounded as if he wasn't married to the boy's mother, although the boy had your father's name."

Pop's face swam in front of him. "You mean—the kid's name was *Patrick McGinnis*? Like Dad?"

"As far as we know." Pop's callused hand settled on his knee. He handed Brandon a napkin and waited while he wiped his eyes. "The boy's mother refused to leave Canada. Your dad came home anyway. Then she disappeared."

The buzzing in Brandon's ears wouldn't quit. "So the guy hasn't heard his father is dead."

"Not yet. The lawyer has tried to find him—but no luck. Your mom has been so upset ever since she found out—she can't talk about it. And she thought the truth would destroy you." Pop's blue eyes were huge behind his glasses. "I decided you ought to know, even though I knew you'd hate the messenger."

Brandon winced. What could he say? He *was* mad at Pop, even though it wasn't his fault.

Pop sighed. "This whole trip was such a bad idea. I never even found Sam's grave."

Brandon set his mug down. "What are you talking about?"

"It was raining so hard—and I was too stubborn to bring my cane—I just wandered all over the damn place."

Brandon grinned. The rum was making him light-headed and warm all at once. "Okay, Pop. Tomorrow's a new day. We'll start from scratch."

They reached the cemetery soon after it opened. In the little building where the registry was kept, they looked up Sam Friedman, then walked arm in arm down the central path. Row upon row of white marble crosses covered the grassy bluff as far as Brandon could see, each one equidistant to the next. It was strangely beautiful and solemn.

And they weren't all crosses. Every once in a while a Star of David marked a grave. Of course, he should have known—Sam Friedman's grave, at the end of the row closest to the sea, was topped with a star. His name, the dates of his birth and death, and his hometown—Brooklyn, New York—were etched into the marble.

Pop stood tall beside the grave, his hand gripping the star's point. "Take my picture," he said in a gruff voice. "I'll send it to his sister."

Brandon snapped a few shots, then moved away when Pop asked for a minute alone. He walked slowly to the edge of the bluff, where he leaned against a cypress tree, letting the rough bark hold him up. Sea and sky were the same quiet gray. He breathed deep. The guys behind him were all underground, finished—like Dad. But he was still here. Why?

To find his brother, Brandon told himself. He'd always hated being an only child. He'd have to search all of Canada for Patrick McGinnis—if that was still his name. He'd look for a guy with those famous green eyes. Of course, if his brother had Dad's pitching arm, he'd hate him for sure. Brandon smiled. Too soon for sibling rivalry.

He turned away from the sea and walked among the graves, forcing himself to confront the dead. Pop saw him coming, and held out his hands.

Liza Ketchum

The spring of 1968 was a chaotic time for America. The Vietnam War raged in Southeast Asia, leading to antiwar protests around the country; Martin Luther King Jr. was assassinated; riots erupted in many cities; and in June, Bobby Kennedy would be murdered in California.

I was a senior in college, working on a short story that was due before graduation. Although I had marched against the war and played peace songs on my guitar, my story was about a woman who worked in a fire tower in the Adirondack Mountains. Like me, she watched the flames from a safe distance.

Then one morning the phone rang in my dormitory room and the war was no longer remote. Mike Ransom, a close childhood friend, had been killed in Vietnam. Mike's cornflower blue eyes had been filled with fear when he'd said good-bye. Now he was dead after being ambushed and mortally wounded on night patrol.

Eight months later my cousin Eddie, a marine helicopter pilot, was shot down while rescuing wounded soldiers. Eddie and I had lived next door to each other growing up. We loved each other—and fought—like brother and sister. Eddie introduced me to rock and roll, taught me to jitterbug, teased me about boys. How could he be gone? The safe, protected world of my childhood disappeared forever. Mike's and Eddie's deaths split my family and our friends into two camps. One group opposed the war and thought these talented young men had died in vain; the others believed the war was a just cause.

Sables Mouvants   **161**

In the fall of 1998 my husband and I visited the cemetery in Normandy dedicated to the American men of World War II who died fighting a so-called good war. As I walked among the silent graves my mind circled back thirty years. I was in Arlington National Cemetery again, feeling the shock of the twenty-one-gun salute as they lowered my cousin into his grave, watching my uncle's hands tremble as he accepted the American flag from his son's coffin. Standing among fallen men from my father's generation, I decided to write a story about the events that divided families in the troubled years of the 1960s.

In my books for young people, I'm interested in the pull of history and the tug one generation exerts on the next. I often write to explore questions I can't answer myself, such as: What happens when a young person tells the truth—and risks tearing a family apart? (*Blue Coyote*); Is it possible to stand up to one's peers—and still survive? (*Twelve Days in August*); What does "family" mean, and who belongs? (*Fire in the Heart; Dancing on the Table*); How did the real people of the past shape the present? (*The Gold Rush*). And with Brandon's story I posed the question that haunts every generation: *Is* there such a thing as a "good" war?

I still don't know the answer.

After a few minutes of drawing, Jack flipped carefully through the notebook and counted the sketches he'd done of her since September. There were fifty-eight.

He glanced back at the girl—the real one, not the picture. The green T-shirt guy was kind of poking at her shoulder, playfully, but it looked as if she was getting annoyed.

Jack tightened his grip on the pen, holding it differently now, the way you would grip it if you were about to jab someone in the temple.

Steppin' Eddie

by Rich Wallace

Jack pushed back his hair and gasped. His forehead was the color and texture of pale bologna. And worse, disgustingly worse, were the slices of olive and pimiento embedded in the skin.

He woke abruptly. He leaped out of bed and rushed to his mirror. He pushed back his hair and let out his breath. No olive slices. No splotches of red. A few zits, as usual. But no olive slices.

They'd had olive loaf for dinner last night, he and his grandmother. Olive loaf sandwiches with mayonnaise. Jack had bought it at the deli on Main Street after sweeping up at the barbershop, where he worked an hour a day after school.

It must have been that he'd been thinking about that olive loaf, subconsciously, and it had intruded on his dreams. Jack realized this suddenly. He went to brush his teeth.

Today was Tuesday, a school day. He had a half hour until the bus came. Most kids his age didn't ride the bus any longer. They had cars, or friends with cars, or they lived close enough that they just walked to school.

165

Jack lived almost two miles from school, in his grandmother's house, in the room that his father had grown up in. Jack had lived his whole life in that house. They lived on six acres, not quite a farm. But definitely not in town.

Jack had a job after school for one hour a day, sweeping up at the barbershop and cleaning the bathroom. Then he walked home with his long, loping strides, his odd, forward-leaning, loose-kneed gait, arriving at about six thirty every evening, which was after dark this time of year.

Jack wore his father's old clothes, which fit him fine. His grandmother still had nearly all of Jack's father's clothes and had kept them in labeled paper bags. Now all of the clothes were out of the bags because Jack was big enough for all of the clothes.

They had a TV but no cable, so they had a choice of three fuzzy channels from Scranton—PBS, CBS, and Fox. No MTV or ESPN. They had no computer or VCR or Nintendo or CD player. Jack had his father's record player in his room, and four of his father's records. One was Bob Dylan (*Highway 61 Revisited*) and another was also Bob Dylan (*Blonde on Blonde*). Another was *Meet the Beatles.* The one he hardly ever listened to was by the Beach Boys.

Jack's father had been in Montana, or somewhere out there, ever since the accident. His mother was in Florida, and Jack hadn't seen her since he was four. He got cards from her sometimes, like every other Christmas. It was like having a distant aunt in Florida, and like having a distant uncle out West. Jack didn't miss his parents.

Jack's grandfather used to say that Jack's father was shiftless and lazy and ignorant. That's why Grandpa'd taken Jack away from him. Jack's father said Grandpa's interference and malevolence had driven Jack's mother away.

Grandpa had died in a hunting accident when Jack was ten. Ask any game warden in Pennsylvania and they'll tell you—you'll lose a dozen or more hunters every deer season to heart attacks or others' poor aim.

Jack didn't miss his grandfather either.

This morning Jack set the volume low and placed the needle on "Till There Was You." He chose the green-and-yellow checked shirt from the closet and the brown corduroy trousers.

In algebra Mr. Sully was explaining square footage. Two boys who sat near the front in the row next to Jack were acting as if they did not get it, but Jack believed that they did. The one fellow with a denim shirt unbuttoned halfway down and a scar on his lower lip was asking how, if a room was nine feet long and six feet wide, it could have any square feet, since it wasn't square at all.

The other one agreed. He had stringy hair down to his shoulders and wore old work boots with no laces in them.

Jack glanced again at the boy with the denim shirt, imagining what the scar would look like freshly reopened, deeper and longer and life threatening.

The two kept on about the square-foot thing for several minutes, until Mr. Sully told them to make an appointment for extra help after school. A man could only take so much.

Jack did understand square footage, so he was sketching a portrait of Mr. Sully. The teacher had a thin face with a high forehead and dark-rimmed glasses and a rubbery mouth.

Jack did not draw very well, but he could capture the essence of a person in his sketches. Often when he came across a picture he'd drawn weeks before, he could recognize who it was!

In study hall the girl across from him was talking about basketball. She was on the team. She had ropy brown hair, braided and pulled back, and nice teeth. The guy she was talking to was sitting backward in his seat to talk to her better. He was wearing a faded green T-shirt that he filled out pretty well, and had short, dark hair and a confident half smile all the time.

These two were friends, not boyfriend and girlfriend. The boy was flirting, but she was deflecting every innuendo. "Get real," Jack heard her say. She had a confident half smile too.

Jack had friends. But it had been about six years since anyone had been to his house, and about six years since he'd been to anyone else's house. It had probably been four years since he'd spoken to anyone his age. So maybe he didn't have any friends after all.

Jack took out his notebook and turned to the back, where he did his sketches. He started to draw the girl with the nice teeth, holding the pen deftly, like an artist, being careful not to let her see him gazing at her out of one corner of an eye. *Hello,* he could almost hear himself saying. *My name is Jack.*

I'm Alicia, she'd say with a warm, inviting smile. *Nice to meet you.*

After a few minutes of drawing, Jack flipped carefully through the notebook and counted the sketches he'd done of her since September. There were fifty-eight.

He glanced back at the girl—the real one, not the picture. The green T-shirt guy was kind of poking at her shoulder, playfully, but it looked as if she was getting annoyed.

Jack tightened his grip on the pen, holding it differently now, the way you would grip it if you were about to jab someone in the temple.

Today there was Salisbury steak for lunch, which was one of Jack's favorites. He took his tray of chopped meat with gravy, peas, a carton of whole milk, and a slice of white bread and set it on a table in the corner of the cafeteria. A couple of tables away two boys, both wearing blue Sturbridge Soccer sweatshirts, acknowledged him.

"Steppin' Eddie," said the one boy, nodding to him.

"STEPPin' EDDDDDDDDie," said the other boy, pointing at Jack, drawing out the first syllables and kind of growling out the name.

Jack grinned and blushed and half raised his right hand, spreading out the fingers in a kind of wave. The boy who accented the syllables was the one who'd started calling him that odd name recently. He shouted it each night as Jack loped by on his way home, on the nearly two-mile walk to his grandmother's house after sweeping the floor at the barbershop. Jack scooted by each night with his odd, high-stepped gait, across the street from where the boy sat. The boy had bad skin and was among the group that loitered on Main Street every evening.

For dinner Jack and his grandmother sat on the couch with cheese sandwiches and watched the seven o'clock news. A Dunmore man had been arrested for threatening his neighbor with a chain saw. In Carbondale, residents were upset over traffic problems caused by a delay in cleaning up after a water main break. And students at the University of Scranton were rallying in protest over a proposed tuition hike.

All of that seemed a world away to Jack, who had only been to the valley twice—once to the Everhart Museum on a fourth-grade field trip, and once to a Red Barons baseball game with the Methodist Youth Fellowship.

Jack paid attention when the sports guy came on, because he mentioned high school basketball. "At ten we'll have all the scores from the first big night of boys' and girls' action," the sportscaster was saying.

Jack had never been to a high school basketball game but thought he might drop in on one soon. His grandmother, who was short and fat, asked Jack if he would like another sandwich. Jack, who was tall and thin, decided that yes, he would.

Jack liked to read before going to sleep. Tonight he took the hefty *Walt Disney's Story Land* treasury from the shelf by his bed and thumbed past "Davy Crockett," "Pluto Pup Goes to Sea," "Babes in Toyland," "The Sorcerer's Apprentice." It was just a week after Thanksgiving, and he still had a warm kind of feeling inside from that holiday. So he turned to "Pilgrim's Party." He'd read about Mickey Mouse and Donald Duck's visit to Plymouth many times before but never grew tired of it.

Tonight his mind was wandering as Mickey tried to carve the Thanksgiving turkey, so Jack set aside the book. The girl with the ropy brown hair was a sophomore, a year behind him.

Hello, my name is Jack, Jack pictured himself saying.

I'm Alicia, she'd say with a sunny smile. *Nice to meet you.* Jack didn't know if her name was Alicia, but it seemed to fit her.

Next he would say something witty and bright, maybe teasing in a way, or flirtatious.

Get real, she would reply, but her laugh would be inviting.

Jack wondered if his grandmother would mind if he turned on the record player. He set the volume so he could just barely hear it, and listened as Paul McCartney sang "Till There Was You" one more time.

Tomorrow he would wear the light blue shirt with the anchor on the pocket. He would work on his confident half smile.

Jack settled into his bed, and soon he was asleep. But at eleven fifty he woke up again from another olive-loaf forehead dream, his skin dotted with little bits of pimiento, looking like spatters of blood.

He turned toward the window. The woods were dark. He wanted to go deep into those woods, out where the accident had occurred. Out where no one could hear him, where he could scream Alicia's name at the top of his lungs, or maybe just whisper to her what he knew.

Jack had been along that night, six years ago, a week after Halloween. He shouldn't have been out there jack-lighting deer, because he was only ten, with bony arms and a stammer. His father and grandfather shouldn't have been out there either, because deer season was three weeks away yet.

They'd been drinking all day, the men, and arguing since lunch. Grandpa said Jack's father's ex-wife was a whore, and Jack's father called Grandpa a wife beater. Grandpa said Jack's father was dumb as a rock, and said Jack would probably turn out the same. They said all this right in front of Jack, which was okay because Jack had heard it before.

Back then Jack's father worked at a hardware store down in Sturbridge and lived above a pizza place on Main Street. He said Jack's grandfather had kicked him out, treated him like shit all his life, and cost him his marriage and his kid. Grandpa countered that Jack's father was a liar and a cheat and couldn't be trusted to keep the boy fed and bathed and respectable.

They kept this up all afternoon, drinking cans of Genesee and even spitting at each other a couple of times. When it got dark, Jack's grandfather chuckled like he always did and said, "We sure are a sorry-assed bunch." But Jack's father didn't even smile.

They took Jack along with them. Deer were easy to find.

Jack's father's aim was terrible in the dark, especially after all that drinking.

Rich Wallace

I was the kind of guy who hung out on the Boulevard with my friends in the evening after track practice, watching buses go by on their way into New York City, busting one another's chops about every little failing in our lives, like the way one guy's father spent all his free time at the Terrace Tavern, or how another had an unconscious habit of sniffing his own armpits repeatedly, or how I'd managed to alienate just about every girl I'd ever been interested in through various and pathetic oversteps.

There was a guy, a year older than us, who would walk by frequently, always on the other side of the street, always in a hurry, always with these goofy, long, high-stepping strides. No one knew him. He'd arrived in town sometime during high school, long after groupings and cliques had been established, and apparently didn't have the ability to break into any of them. You'd just see him, with regular frequency, walking oddly by.

He'd been dubbed "Footstepper"—just because of the way he walked—by that kind of collective small-town cleverness that pulls nicknames out of the air and makes them stick. We knew nothing about him except the way he looked and the way he walked. But I've often wondered. So I gave him a small role in my second novel, *Shots on Goal*. Footstepper just walks past in that book, the way he did in real life, with a sheepish smile and somewhere to get to in a hurry.

Here he is again, in this story, renicknamed Steppin' Eddie by a kid who could have been me or one of my friends. Or some other guy who should have got to know him for real.

Rich Wallace is the author of two novels: *Wrestling Sturbridge*, which was a 1997 American Library Association Best Book for Young Adults, and *Shots on Goal*, which *Booklist* selected as one of the top ten youth sports books of the year. Both books are set in the imaginary town of Sturbridge, Pennsylvania. Sturbridge draws its life from the real town of Honesdale, Pennsylvania, where Mr. Wallace lives with his two sons. He works as an editor at *Highlights for Children* magazine and plays basketball with a frequency bordering on obsession.

Inch by inch Vinny made it to the ledge. He stood, swaying slightly, the tips of his toes one small movement from the precipice.

Far below, Joe-Boy waved his arm back and forth. It was dreamy to see—back and forth, back and forth. He looked so small down there.

For a moment Vinny's mind went blank, as if he were in some trance, some dream where he could so easily lean out and fall, and think or feel nothing.

A breeze picked up and moved the trees on the ridgeline, but not a breath of it reached the fifty-foot ledge.

Vinny thought he heard a voice, small and distant. Yes. Something inside him, a tiny voice pleading, Don't do it. Walk away. Just turn and go and walk back down.

"... I can't," Vinny whispered.

The Ravine

by Graham Salisbury

When Vinny and three others dropped down into the ravine, they entered a jungle thick with tangled trees and rumors of what might have happened to the dead boy's body.

The muddy trail was slick and, in places where it had fallen away, flat-out dangerous. The cool breeze that swept the Hawaiian hillside pastures above died early in the descent.

There were four of them—Vinny; his best friend, Joe-Boy; Mo, who was afraid of nothing; and Joe-Boy's *haole* girlfriend, Starlene—all fifteen. It was a Tuesday in July, two weeks and a day after the boy had drowned. If, in fact, that's what had happened to him.

Vinny slipped, and dropped his towel in the mud. He picked it up and tried to brush it off, but instead smeared the mud spot around until the towel resembled something someone's dog had slept on. "Tst," he said.

Joe-Boy, hiking down just behind him, laughed. "Hey, Vinny, just think, that kid walked where you walking."

"Shuddup," Vinny said.

179

"You prob'ly stepping right where his foot was."

Vinny moved to the edge of the trail, where the ravine fell through a twisted jungle of gnarly trees and underbrush to the stream far below.

Joe-Boy laughed again. "You such a queen, Vinny. You know that?"

Vinny could see Starlene and Mo farther ahead, their heads bobbing as they walked, both almost down to the pond where the boy had died.

"Hey," Joe-Boy went on, "maybe you going be the one to find his body."

"You don't cut it out, Joe-Boy, I going . . . I going . . ."

"What, cry?"

Vinny scowled. Sometimes Joe-Boy was a big fat babooze.

They slid down the trail. Mud oozed between Vinny's toes. He grabbed at roots and branches to keep from falling. Mo and Starlene were out of sight now, the trail ahead having cut back.

Joe-Boy said, "You going jump in the water and go down and your hand going touch his face, stuck under the rocks. *Ha ha ha . . . a ha ha ha!*"

Vinny winced. He didn't want to be here. It was too soon, way too soon. Two weeks and one day.

He saw a footprint in the mud and stepped around it.

The dead boy had jumped and had never come back up. Four search and rescue divers hunted for two days straight and never found him. Not a trace. Gave Vinny the creeps. It didn't make sense. The pond wasn't that big.

He wondered why it didn't seem to bother anyone else. Maybe it did and they just didn't want to say.

Butchie was the kid's name. Only fourteen.

Fourteen.

Two weeks and one day ago he was walking down this trail. Now nobody could find him.

The jungle crushed in, reaching over the trail, and Vinny brushed leafy branches aside. The roar of the waterfall got louder, louder.

Starlene said it was the goddess that took him, the one that lives in the stone down by the road. She did that every now and then, Starlene said, took somebody when she got lonely. Took him and kept him. Vinny had heard that legend before, but he'd never believed in it.

Now he didn't know what he believed.

The body had to be stuck down there. But still, four divers and they couldn't find it?

Vinny decided he'd better believe in the legend. If he didn't, the goddess might get mad and send him bad luck. Or maybe take *him,* too.

Stopstopstop! Don't think like that.

"Come on," Joe-Boy said, nudging Vinny from behind. "Hurry it up."

Just then Starlene whooped, her voice bouncing around the walls of the ravine.

"Let's *go,*" Joe-Boy said. "They there already."

Moments later, Vinny jumped up onto a large boulder at the edge of the pond. Starlene was swimming out in the brown water. It wasn't murky brown, but clean and clear to a depth of maybe three or four feet. Because of the waterfall you had to yell if you wanted to say something. The whole place smelled of mud and ginger and iron.

Starlene swam across to the waterfall on the far side of the pond and ducked under it, then climbed out and edged along the rock wall behind it, moving slowly, like a spider. Above, sun-sparkling stream water spilled over the lip of a one-hundred-foot drop.

Mo and Joe-Boy threw their towels onto the rocks and dove into the pond. Vinny watched, his muddy towel hooked around his neck. Reluctantly, he let it fall, then dove in after them.

The cold mountain water tasted tangy. Was it because the boy's body was down there decomposing? He spit it out.

He followed Joe-Boy and Mo to the waterfall and ducked under it. They climbed up onto the rock ledge, just as Starlene had done, then spidered their way over to where you could climb to a small ledge about fifteen feet up. They took their time because the hand and footholds were slimy with moss.

Starlene jumped first. Her shriek echoed off the rocky cliff, then died in the dense green jungle.

Mo jumped, then Joe-Boy, then Vinny.

The fifteen-foot ledge was not the problem.

It was the one above it, the one you had to work up to, the big one, where you had to take a deadly zigzag trail that climbed up and away from the waterfall, then cut back and forth to a foot-wide ledge something more like fifty feet up.

That was the problem.

That was where the boy had jumped from.

Joe-Boy and Starlene swam out to the middle of the pond. Mo swam back under the waterfall and climbed once again to the fifteen-foot ledge.

Vinny started to swim out toward Joe-Boy but stopped when he saw Starlene put her arms around him. She kissed him. They sank under for a long time, then came back up, still kissing.

Joe-Boy saw Vinny looking and winked. "You like that, Vinny? Watch, I show you how." He kissed Starlene again.

Vinny turned away and swam back over to the other side of the pond, where he'd first gotten in. His mother would kill him if she ever heard about where he'd come. After the boy drowned, or was taken by the goddess, or whatever happened to him, she said never to come to this pond again. Ever. It was off-limits. Permanently.

But not his dad. He said, "You fall off a horse, you get back on, right? Or else you going be scared of it all your life."

His mother scoffed and waved him off. "Don't listen to him, Vinny, listen to me. Don't go there. That pond is haunted." Which had made his dad laugh.

But Vinny promised he'd stay away.

But then Starlene and Joe-Boy said, "Come with us anyway. You let your mommy run your life, or what?" And Vinny said, "But what if I get caught?" And Joe-Boy said, "So?"

Vinny mashed his lips. He was so weak. Couldn't even say no. But if he'd said, "I can't go, my mother won't like it," they would have laughed him right off the island. No, he had to go. No choice.

So he'd come along, and so far it was fine. He'd even gone in the water. Everyone was happy. All he had to do now was wait it out and go home and hope his mother never heard about it.

When he looked up, Starlene was gone.

He glanced around the pond until he spotted her starting up the zigzag trail to the fifty-foot ledge. She was moving slowly, hanging on to roots and branches on the upside of the cliff. He couldn't believe she was going there. He wanted to yell, *Hey, Starlene, that's where he died!*

But she already knew that.

Mo jumped from the lower ledge, yelling, "Banzaiiii!" An explosion of coffee-colored water erupted when he hit.

Joe-Boy swam over to where Starlene had gotten out. He waved to Vinny, grinning like a fool, then followed Starlene up the zigzag trail.

Now Starlene was twenty-five, thirty feet up. Vinny watched her for a while, then lost sight of her when she slipped behind a wall of jungle that blocked his view. A few minutes later she popped back out, now almost at the top, where the trail ended, where there was nothing but mud and a few plants to grab on to if you slipped, plants that would rip right out of the ground, plants that wouldn't stop you if you fell, nothing but your screams between you and the rocks below.

Vinny's stomach tingled just watching her. He couldn't imagine what it must feel like to be up there, especially if you were afraid of heights, like he was. *She has no fear,* Vinny thought, *no fear at all. Pleasepleaseplease, Starlene. I don't want to see you die.*

Starlene crept forward, making her way to the end of the trail, where the small ledge was.

Joe-Boy popped out of the jungle behind her. He stopped, waiting for her to jump before going on.

Vinny held his breath.

Starlene, in her cutoff jeans and soaked T-shirt, stood perfectly still, her arms at her sides. Vinny suddenly felt like hugging her. Why, he couldn't tell. *Starlene, please.*

She reached behind her and took a wide leaf from a plant, then eased down and scooped up a finger of mud. She made a brown cross on her forehead, then wiped her muddy fingers on her jeans.

She waited.

Was she thinking about the dead boy?

She stuck the stem end of the leaf in her mouth, leaving the rest of it to hang out. When she jumped, the leaf would flap up and cover her nose and keep water from rushing into it. An old island trick.

She jumped.

Down, down.

Almost in slow motion, it seemed at first, then faster and faster. She fell feetfirst, arms flapping to keep balance so she wouldn't land on her back, or stomach, which would probably almost kill her.

Just before she hit, she crossed her arms over her chest and vanished within a small explosion of rusty water.

Vinny stood, not breathing at all, praying.

Ten seconds. Twenty, thirty . . .

She came back up, laughing.

She shouldn't make fun that way, Vinny thought. It was dangerous, disrespectful. It was asking for it.

Vinny looked up when he heard Joe-Boy shout, "Hey, Vinny, watch how a man does it! Look!"

Joe-Boy scooped up some mud and drew a stroke of lightning across his chest. When he jumped, he threw himself out, face and body parallel to the pond, his arms and legs spread out. *He's crazy,* Vinny thought, *absolutely insane.* At the last second Joe-Boy folded into a ball and hit. *Ca-roomp!* He came up whooping and yelling, "*Wooo!* So *good!* Come on, Vinny, it's hot!"

Vinny faked a laugh. He waved, shouting, "Naah, the water's too cold!"

Now Mo was heading up the zigzag trail—Mo, who hardly ever said a word and would do anything anyone ever challenged him to do. *Come on, Mo, not you, too.*

Vinny knew then that he would have to jump.

Jump, or never live it down.

Mo jumped in the same way Joe-Boy had, man-style, splayed out in a suicide fall. He came up grinning.

Starlene and Joe-Boy turned toward Vinny.

Vinny got up and hiked around the edge of the pond, walking in the muddy shallows, looking at a school of small brown-backed fish near a ginger patch.

Maybe they'd forget about him.

Starlene torpedoed over, swimming underwater. Her body glittered in the small amount of sunlight that penetrated the trees around the rim of the ravine. When she came up, she broke the surface smoothly, gracefully, like a swan. Her blond hair sleeked back like river grass.

She smiled a sweet smile. "Joe-Boy says you're afraid to jump. I didn't believe him. He's wrong, right?"

Vinny said quickly, "Of course he's wrong. I just don't want to, that's all. The water's cold."

"Naah, it's nice."

Vinny looked away. On the other side of the pond Joe-Boy and Mo were on the cliff behind the waterfall.

"Joe-Boy says your mom told you not to come here. Is that true?"

Vinny nodded. "Yeah. Stupid, but she thinks it's haunted."

"She's right."

"What?"

"That boy didn't die, Vinny. The stone goddess took him. He's in a good place right now. He's her prince."

Vinny scowled. He couldn't tell if Starlene was teasing him or if she really believed that. He said, "Yeah, prob'ly."

"Are you going to jump, or is Joe-Boy right?"

"Joe-Boy's an idiot. Sure I'm going to jump."

Starlene grinned, staring at Vinny a little too long. "He is an idiot, isn't he? But I love him."

"Yeah, well . . ."

"Go to it, big boy. I'll be watching."

Starlene sank down and swam out into the pond.

Ca-ripes.

Vinny ripped a hank of white ginger from the ginger

patch and smelled it, and prayed he'd still be alive after the sun went down.

He took his time climbing the zigzag trail. When he got to the part where the jungle hid him from view, he stopped and smelled the ginger again. So sweet and alive it made Vinny wish for all he was worth that he was climbing out of the ravine right now, heading home.

But of course, there was no way he could do that.

Not before jumping.

He tossed the ginger onto the muddy trail and continued on. He slipped once or twice, maybe three times. He didn't keep track. He was too numb now, too caught up in the insane thing he was about to do. He'd never been this far up the trail before. Once he'd tried to go all the way, but couldn't. It made him dizzy.

When he stepped out and the jungle opened into a huge bowl where he could look down, way, way down, he could see there three heads in the water, heads with arms moving slowly to keep them afloat, and a few bright rays of sunlight pouring down onto them, and when he saw this, his stomach fluttered and rose. Something sour came up and he spit it out.

It made him wobble to look down. He closed his eyes. His whole body trembled. The trail was no wider than the length of his foot. And it was wet and muddy from little rivulets of water that bled from the side of the cliff.

The next few steps were the hardest he'd ever taken in his life. He tried not to look down, but he couldn't help it. His gaze was drawn there. He struggled to push back an urge to fly, just jump off and fly. He could almost see himself spiraling down like a glider, or a bird, or a leaf.

His hands shook as if he were freezing. He wondered, *Had the dead boy felt this way?* Or had he felt brave, like Starlene or Joe-Boy, or Mo, who seemed to feel nothing.

Somebody from below shouted, but Vinny couldn't make it out over the waterfall, roaring down just feet beyond the ledge where he would soon be standing, cascading past so close its mist dampened the air he breathed.

The dead boy had just come to the ravine to have fun, Vinny thought. Just a regular kid like himself, come to swim and be with his friends, then go home and eat macaroni and cheese and watch TV, maybe play with his dog or wander around after dark.

But he'd done none of that.

Where was he?

Inch by inch Vinny made it to the ledge. He stood, swaying slightly, the tips of his toes one small movement from the precipice.

Far below, Joe-Boy waved his arm back and forth. It was dreamy to see—back and forth, back and forth. He looked so small down there.

For a moment Vinny's mind went blank, as if he were in some trance, some dream where he could so easily lean out and fall, and think or feel nothing.

A breeze picked up and moved the trees on the ridgeline, but not a breath of it reached the fifty-foot ledge.

Vinny thought he heard a voice, small and distant. Yes. Something inside him, a tiny voice pleading, *Don't do it. Walk away. Just turn and go and walk back down.*

"... I can't," Vinny whispered.

You can, you can, you can. Walk back down.

Vinny waited.

And waited.

Joe-Boy yelled, then Starlene, both of them waving.

Then something very strange happened.

Vinny felt at peace. Completely and totally calm and at peace. He had not made up his mind about jumping. But something else inside him had.

Thoughts and feelings swarmed, stinging him: *Jump! Jump! Jump! Jump!*

But deep inside, where the peace was, where his mind wasn't, he would not jump. He would walk back down.

No! No, no, no!

Vinny eased down and fingered up some mud and made a cross on his chest, big and bold. He grabbed a leaf, stuck it in his mouth. *Be calm, be calm. Don't look down.*

After a long pause he spit the leaf out and rubbed the cross to a blur.

They walked out of the ravine in silence, Starlene, Joe-Boy, and Mo far ahead of him. They hadn't said a word since he'd come down off the trail. He knew what they were thinking. He knew, he knew, he knew.

At the same time the peace was still there. He had no idea what it was. But he prayed it wouldn't leave him now, prayed it wouldn't go away, would never go away, because in there, in that place where the peace was, it didn't matter what they thought.

Vinny emerged from the ravine into a brilliance that surprised him. Joe-Boy, Starlene, and Mo were now almost down to the road.

Vinny breathed deeply, and looked up and out over the island. He saw, from there, a land that rolled away like honey, easing down a descent of rich Kikuyu grass pasture-land, flowing from there over vast highlands of brown and green, then, finally, falling massively to the coast and flat blue sea.

He'd never seen anything like it.

Had it always been here? This view of the island?

He stared and stared, then sat, taking it in.

He'd never seen anything so beautiful in all his life.

Graham Salisbury

I was surfing one day with a friend and two others guys. This was back in my kid days in Hawaii. I was fourteen.

We were sitting on our boards over a shallow reef, waiting for a set of decent waves. The water was smooth and pristine, so clear you could see each individual spike of every stinging black *wana* on the coral below. It was heaven.

One of the guys motioned with his chin off to our right. We looked. A shark fin, leisurely cutting the surface.

Ca-ripes, I thought.

The fin vanished.

I sat up straighter, looked around, wondering where the dang thing was. I wanted to pull up my feet, which were dangling off my board. I wanted to paddle in, get out of the water. I didn't want to be some shark's lunch.

Did I?

Nope.

The shark came up again, this time to our left. Jeez! It must have gone under us. Maybe it had even sniffed my toes! Did any of the other guys look nervous? Nope. Did I look nervous? I tried very hard not to. Was I nervous? Oh, yeah.

Now did anyone get out of the water?

Not on your life.

Why?

Because we were idiots. Too vain to be the first to get scared enough to make a break for shore. So we just sat there like invincible fools. Sheese.

"The Ravine" is my tribute to every young person on the edge of making an intelligent decision. I know it doesn't always happen. But I also know it's not impossible. As a writer I've met a lot of truly fine young people. And a few invincible fools, too.

Graham Salisbury's books include *Blue Skin of the Sea, Under the Blood-Red Sun, Shark Bait,* and *Jungle Dogs.* He also has stories in several short story anthologies. Among his awards and honors are the Scott O'Dell Historical Fiction Award, Hawaii's Nene Award, the California Young Reader Medal, the Judy Lopez Award, the Parents' Choice Award, the Bank Street College Child Study Children's Book Committee Children's Book Award, the Oregon Book Award, an American Library Association Best Book for Young Adults, a *School Library Journal* Best Book of the Year, a *Booklist* Editors' Choice, the Family Channel Seal of Quality, and the PEN/Norma Klein Award.

The roar of the river grows. And up ahead light blooms like a white blossom opening.

Yee halts ten meters from the edge of the light. The Hmong cannot be seen, but they can see to the opening of the trench and to the sky beyond. Yee feels the weight of the souls behind him. The roar of the river shakes the foliage overhead, the sides of the trench, the floor.

The Pathet Lao patrol enters the trench. The soldiers squint into the darkness. They advance.

In the Valley of Elephants

by Terry Davis

The Mouas, that family of Hmong people, they didn't always own American Video near the corner of Hamilton and Dakota in Spokane.

FADE IN:

A white dot swirls in darkness. It grows. It is a flower opening.

In the darkness a baby cries.

Dissolve to a Laotian forest, day, where a Hmong woman with a toddler on her hip and an infant strapped to her breast crouches in a shallow trench two meters wide. This is an elephant trench, and it runs through the Valley of Elephants in northcentral Laos. Decades have passed since elephants walked this trail, and hundreds of years since they wore it deep and wide. Even so, a sense of their density and power remains. Sometimes the trench walls expand and contract in the shadows like the breathing of a great gray chest. Most of the elephants in Laos are dead, casualties of the U.S. bombing. The year is 1975. For America the war is over.

The woman, May Moua, seventeen, presses herself

against the trench wall, her face a few centimeters from a white flower, big as a softball, growing on a vine. May cannot stifle the baby's cries.

A line of Hmong women, children, and old people stretches behind May, eastward, out of the trench and into the forest shadows.

A man in the uniform of the Pathet Lao, the Laotian communist army, steps out of the forest. He looks down into the trench, waving his rifle like a death wand up and down the line of fearful people. Then he takes one hand off the rifle and pulls a grenade from his belt. He lets the rifle hang on its sling as he takes a step back and moves to pull the pin.

But there's a blur and a *whoosh* as something strikes him from the foliage. And a soft *thunk* as steel cleaves flesh and embeds itself in bone.

Yee Moua, nineteen, wearing a Fiat shop coat, slips a machete into its scabbard. Yee was a Fiat mechanic, and he may be again if he can get these people to the Mekong River, across it, and into Thailand.

Yee kneels and takes the Pathet Lao's weapons, covers the body with vines—one of which holds the white flower—and jumps down into the trench.

All along the line men join their families. None is in uniform, but most carry sophisticated weapons. One man who carries only a garden hoe receives the Pathet Lao's rifle and ammunition pouch.

Yee takes the older child from May. The infant is still crying.

YEE: You've got to keep the baby quiet. The
Pathet Lao are everywhere.

MAY: I'm afraid. When I cover her mouth, I'm
afraid she'll suffocate.

Yee hands her a corked bottle from his breast pocket. The oily liquid washes into the bottle's neck and leaves a film.

YEE: The opium will put her to sleep.

MAY: If I give her too much, she'll never wake up.

YEE: Don't give her too much. The elephant
trench runs for miles. When night falls and the trench
gets deeper, we'll be well hidden. With luck we can
make the river before dawn.

The fear in May's face grows at the words *elephant trench*. She drops the opium. She bends and extends her hand for the bottle, but memory reaches up out of the packed brown dirt, and May jerks away. The bottle of opium remains on the trench floor.

Yee leads the people farther into the trench. It gets deeper until the smooth, concave walls dwarf them as they disappear into the dark forest.

Sunset advances into the rugged mountains to the northeast, an incursion of red, gold, and purple waves leveling the mountaintops and filling the mountain valleys with bristling beauty. These mountains are where May grew up, and where she first heard of an elephant trench.

If May were home gazing out the door of their *jah* at the sunset, her mind's eye would flash to the first stunning moments of a B-52 strike where the colors of the sun boiled up from the earth before smoke and the earth itself veiled them in a dirty rain. May had not been able to turn her eyes from those moments of lethal beauty.

May told no one of her fascination with the air strikes. When her first child was a baby, she would carry him in the evenings to the edge of the village where the slope dropped off into the dark treetops below. Even if the bombs fell so far away that they were silent and the flashes were like the flares of matches, the mountain still trembled, and tremors climbed her legs and moved through her arms into the baby, who would flex his tiny shoulders outward, then turn in on himself again and suck at his thumb and first finger. May would tell herself that one day when she was old—if the bombs didn't fall on her first—she would have a story to tell the children of the village.

Sometimes the bombs fell when the family was asleep. If the strike was close enough, the *jah* shook. Dishes fell. Mice would rain from the thatch roof like soft, furry, ter- rified pears. One night May was sewing when she felt the bombs. A spider was knocked from its web, and she watched it dangle in the golden light of the kerosene lamp. She thought of her father, who had been a wood- cutter and who had more than once fallen from a tree he was topping and been saved by his rope.

When the bombs woke May from sleep, if they were the right distance away, they sounded and felt to her like all the elephants since the beginning of the world pounding a trench through the land on their way to her door.

Dissolve to May's memory, Hmong village, exterior, night, where an old woman tells a story by firelight. The children who sit around the fire are entranced, one little girl in particular.

OLD WOMAN: Once upon a time, thousands of years before the fall of the Hmong kingdom and our journey south, in the morning of the world when a multitude of spirits walked among us, the god-man, Yer Shau, sought to rescue the souls of our ancestors from the savage Ndu Nyong.

Yer Shau's eyes could not abide the sight of the Savage One plucking up handfuls of Hmong from his mountaintop corral and ripping them apart, drinking their cascading blood, feasting on their flesh, crunching their bones in his great jaws; nor could his ears abide the screams. But Yer Shau did not have the strength to break through the weave of redwood logs that formed the corral walls. Only one creature besides the Savage One himself had such strength. And so Yer Shau sought the help of the elephants.

The story spans times and distance. May's fear is the bridge that links the past and present.

In the present, in the elephant trench, May remembers the legend of Yer Shau and the elephants. Her fear grows. The baby has fallen asleep.

In the past, in the village, the story continues:

OLD WOMAN: After feasting on our ancestors, the Savage One fell into his long, deep, gory slumber. Yer Shau crept out of the forest to the corral and peeked between the huge logs. They were as thick as the god-man was tall, and yet Ndu Nyong had woven them like a great straw basket to contain the roiling mass of anguished Hmong souls.

In no time the mountains rang with the Savage One's snores, the wind rose with his foul vapors, and dried Hmong blood encrusted his closed eyes. Before Yer Shau crept back into the forest, he watched the scaly eyelids pulse and flutter like the ripped and dying hearts of our people as the Savage One dreamed his bloody dreams.

Yer Shau marshaled the elephants, led them from their valley and up the rocky trail. Together and by stealth they unthreaded one of the redwood logs from the weave. Together they welcomed the grateful Hmong souls who came pouring out.

The children are captivated. But young May grows more and more fearful. It's not the gore that frightens her. It's the awesome size and strength of the elephants. Yer Shau and Ndu Nyong are make-believe. Elephants are real.

In May's imagination the elephants come alive as the old woman's words ring out in the firelight.

OLD WOMAN: Year after year the elephants walked the trail as allies of Yer Shau and friends of the Hmong. Their thundering feet wore the trail deep, and their great, rolling bellies wore it wide and smooth-sided, until it became as it is today: deep as an elephant is tall and wide as an elephant is round.

The old woman's face shows that she herself is moved by the story.

OLD WOMAN: As the earth wears away, so do all things wear away: The god-man came to our aid less frequently; the helping spirits grew dimmer and dimmer until only our shamans were able to distinguish them; and the elephants dwindled in number. But before these things came to pass, our old friends rose to our aid one final time.

After decades of battle the Chinese had driven us from our mountain villages. But it was not enough for them to have won the land they begrudged us. We had exacted a high price in Chinese lives for our eviction, and they, like the Savage One, thirsted for Hmong blood.

In the present, in the elephant trench, it is a different enemy in 1975, but again the Hmong are fleeing for their lives.

May's fear continues to grow. The baby wakes and begins to cry. May raises it to her face and sings a lullaby in its ear.

In the forest a Pathet Lao patrol advances.

In the distance light rises along the horizon. This could be the people's last morning in Laos, or it could be their last morning in the world. A sound like thunder has risen with the light. To May it is the rumble of elephants.

Massive shapes loom in the gray light. They look like elephants. But they aren't moving.

They *aren't* elephants. They are gigantic boulders. And the roar is the Mekong River working its way around them.

In the elephant trench May's fear assures her that the rumble she hears is elephants. The old woman's voice rains down on her.

OLD WOMAN (voice-over):   The fastest way to safety was through the elephant trench, but it provided a fast route for the Chinese as well. The fleeing Hmong were an entire people—old ones, woman and children, along with the warriors. They were slow. If the Chinese caught them in the trench, they would be slaughtered. But the trench was our only chance. Women and children entered the musty shadows first, then the old ones, and finally the warriors.

Yee lowers the little boy to the ground beside May. The baby is crying hard.

YEE: You must keep the baby quiet, May. We're almost there. In a few minutes the sound of the river will cover everything. But you must keep the baby quiet now. Stay here until I get back.

Yee sees May is edging into hysteria. He whispers in the baby's ear, pulls the blanket more fully around her face, and walks alone into the darkness.

May holds the baby tighter. And the tighter May holds, the harder the tiny girl cries. But May doesn't hear or see the baby. Fear holds May in another place and time.

OLD WOMAN (voice-over):   After night fell, when the elephant trench was dark as Ndu Nyong's stomach, the earth began to tremble. The trembling grew to a quaking that shook the last few teeth from the heads of the old ones. Even the warriors were rendered incontinent and fell weeping to the trench floor. Then the trumpeting began. It rose to such an elevation that the people were made deaf to their own screams and the milk of nursing mothers curdled in their breasts. Such was the people's fear that not a single Hmong eye was lifted to see the end of their days descend.

At the opening of the trench Yee looks out through the foliage.

The sun has risen.

The Mekong thunders around elephant-size boulders. The Pathet Lao patrol walks the river's edge.

Yee turns back toward the trench. The overgrowth is so thick that daylight penetrates only a few meters into the trench. It is like a cave. As Yee hurries back into the darkness he hears the baby crying.

In the trench Yee rejoins the others as a woman puts the wailing baby to May's breast. Instantly the baby quiets. The sound of its urgent nursing rises over the faint rumble of the river.

Yee hoists the little boy on his hip. He speaks to a

In the Valley of Elephants   **205**

man who then passes the word. The group closes ranks and advances.

The roar of the river grows. And up ahead light blooms like a white blossom opening.

Yee halts ten meters from the edge of the light. The Hmong cannot be seen, but they can see to the opening of the trench and to the sky beyond. Yee feels the weight of the souls behind him. The roar of the river shakes the foliage overhead, the sides of the trench, the floor.

The Pathet Lao patrol enters the trench. The soldiers squint into the darkness. They advance.

Yee waits with one knee on the ground and his other leg bent, supporting his son. The little boy's head is buried under Yee's arm. With that hand and his other arm Yee steadies his rifle. It is an AK-47, Russian, a gift from the dead. Yee is a man who appreciates tools, and he has found this tool to be functional, serviceable, durable. Yee is as sure of this Russian carbine as he would be of a screwdriver or a ball-peen hammer.

The Hmong wait. Those in the rear strain for a look into the light, where their fate will be decided.

May squats against the trench wall. She clasps her arms around her knees. She folds inside herself as she would fold a pair of the baby's tiny socks. May is oblivious to the baby, who makes no sound as its thin spine breaks at the base of its neck.

May clinches her eyes. She has always imagined the terror of the Chinese and the gruesome tableau of their deaths more deeply than the triumph of the Hmong. And now that fate has brought her to the elephant trench, she is living that terror. And in all of her senses she is dying that death.

May screams. People jump to shut her up. No one thinks of the baby.

The Pathet Lao advance. They have not heard May over the roar of the river. Two men step from the light into the darkness.

Light outlines the two Pathet Lao soldiers like an eclipse. They wait, then turn and walk away. The rest of the patrol follows.

OLD WOMAN (voice-over):   It was the blood wetting their arms and legs that brought the warriors' heads up, then brought them to their feet, then brought shouts of joy to their lips. This was not the blood of their parents, wives, and children. It was flowing from behind them, from the north. It was the blood of their enemies.

At the opening of the trench Yee looks out.

The Pathet Lao patrol follows the river downstream and out of sight.

The river is narrow and shallow here. The rocks and the wild water create the danger. Yee ties a rope to a rock and fights his way across. He ties the other end to a tree and makes his way back along the rope.

Yee hoists up his son and his rifle, and keeps watch as the Hmong cross the river.

May struggles across with the help of another woman. The baby is swaddled against her chest. There is no reason to think it's not sleeping. May has regained some composure now that she is out of the trench.

Yee and his son are the last to cross. Yee slings his rifle, holds his son with one hand and the rope with the other, and makes his way.

OLD WOMAN (voice-over):   When the Hmong people stood in the sunlight of the Valley of Elephants, they turned to look back at the dark place they had thought would be their grave. At the mouth of the trench stood a great, trumpeting, blood-spattered elephant, and astride its rearing head sat Yer Shau, the god-man, waving his arms and exclaiming victory. And behind him, stretching as far into the distance as the sharpest eye could see, an array of spirits and Hmong souls sat astride the gray heads of elephants, waving and shouting a victorious farewell.

On the Thai side of the Mekong, day, an exhausted and ecstatic group of people greets Yee and the boy as they step out of the water. Everyone hurries for the cover of the forest.

There is much rejoicing. Yee looks for May. When he hears women weeping, his smile broadens as he imagines their tears of joy.

But when he walks back into the sunlight, he sees that joy is not the source of their tears. A desolate wail issues from the circle of women. The circle opens.

May stands with her blouse open, holding the naked baby girl in outstretched arms. The baby has no visible injuries. But her tiny chest is still and the luminescence has faded from her skin.

Yee rushes forward. He puts his son down, and the boy throws his arms around his mother's leg. Yee tries to take the baby, but May won't let her go.

May holds their daughter as Yee cradles the tiny girl's head with the fingertips of one hand. He puts his ear to her chest. It is the chest of a baby bird. He looks at May, who is silent now.

May, Yee, the one living child, and the one dead are framed in a half circle of sorrowful men and women.

May's face shows that the weight of this tiny spirit is hers to carry.

May's face FADES OUT.

Terry Davis

"In the Valley of Elephants" is a chapter from a forthcoming novel titled *The Silk Ball*. It's the story of an eighteen-year-old Hmong high school student who is applying to the screenwriting program at the University of Southern California. His name is Chang Moua; he's a character from one of my earlier novels, *If Rock and Roll Were a Machine*. Much of the book is written in the modified screenplay form I use to present the story.

I learned about the Hmong people when I studied our early involvement in Southeast Asia. They have been known through the centuries as fierce fighters. A friend of mine in Spokane, Keith Quincy, wrote a history of the Hmong, and I learned a great deal more reading that; I also met some of the Hmong who settled in Spokane.

My wife, Becky Davis, is an academic adviser at Minnesota State University–Mankato, where I teach, and Becky works with a lot of Hmong students. I got to know some of these young people, and I came to see their culture as it is here in the States.

The Hmong are an immigrant people. They had a tough life in Laos, and they have a tough life here. No matter how smart or industrious you are, it's tough to come into a new culture and a new language and try to make a life. But so many of these people—the young in particular—are making it. Their lives interest me and touch me, as the lives of any people do when they have come so far and still have so much to endure. So many of these people exemplify the best of the human spirit.

That's what touches me and is why I've chosen a Hmong kid and his dreams to write about.

Terry Davis is a writer and teacher of writing who lives in Mankato, Minnesota. His work includes the novels *Vision Quest*, the story of a high school wrestler, adapted into a film of the same name; *Mysterious Ways*; and *If Rock and Roll Were a Machine*; as well as a Twayne Series biography of the young adult novelist Chris Crutcher. Forthcoming novels include *The Silk Ball*, *A Year in My Father's Country*, and a new edition of *Mysterious Ways*.

Mr. Davis and his wife, Becky—a writer too, who also races bicycles—have four children, ages sixteen through twenty, along with too many dogs, bicycles, and motorcycles for their own good.